I0679960

TWISTED CONTRACT

THE MACNAMARA BROTHERS
BOOK 2

CARINA BLAKE

The Steele Press

ISBN: 978-1-954645-20-2

"What about the baby?" I ask. Our mother gave birth about a week ago to a little boy, and he was the reason she'd been sick. In my opinion no woman her age should be carrying a baby. The risk is too great. Childbirth, although necessary and miraculous, is insanely brutal to a woman and my father knew it. He risked her life for another child like the selfish, arrogant prick that he is.

"You mean our baby brother?" he questions, raising his brows in that unforgiving expression of disapproval. Jack, as the eldest, took being the caretaker of us extremely seriously and that extended to the new addition. He helped raise us and I'm assuming it would be no different with our little brother now.

"Yes, of course. It's not like I forgot John is our brother. It's just—" I hate the thoughts swamping my brain, but my heart is cracked—shattered is more like it.

"If he hadn't been born, Mom would still be alive, but that shit isn't his fault, and you know it." Yes, I do. It's not his fault at all, but I'm being an irrational young man who just lost his mother. What the fuck does Jack expect?

"I expect you to act like a loving brother to an innocent child," he answers. Son of a bitch. I'm such a mess that I'm speaking my thoughts aloud. It's not something someone in my position should do no matter the circumstances. We're not the type of men who can slip up like that. I take a calming breath and attempt to gain my composure.

"Fine. All my hate will be for our father," I state, thinking about his role in this. If he hadn't knocked her up at fifty years old, she wouldn't be gone.

"I never expected anything different." Jack nodded in agreement, but dealing with the old bastard wouldn't be easy because he was still head of this family.

Jack's office door swings open. "I can't believe she's gone." Ian walks in slowly and before we can say a word, he slams his fist through Jack's wall, destroying it like it was paper. He's two years younger than me, but Ian's a muscled beast. He could rip my father's head off, and I'm betting he wants to as much as we do, but there are rules.

Ignoring the splintered wood and plaster, Jack walks over and hands Ian a glass of whiskey.

"I'm sorry," Ian apologizes, tossing back the drink as if he doesn't have busted and bloody knuckles.

"Don't be sorry, Ian. Our mother is gone, and there's nothing we can do about it. Fuck, it's killing me to consider never seeing her beautifully sweet face again," Jack says. He might be the oldest and my father's right-hand man, but that doesn't eliminate him from the pain of losing our mother. His eyes are red-rimmed as he tries to remain tough.

I pour myself a drink and toss it back in one long gulp. She'd been out of the hospital and back home for only two days before they rushed her back in.

"As am I," Nick says, coming up to my side and kissing my cheek. I do my best not to shy away—not let everyone see my revulsion. He slides his hand around my waist as the dinner party gathers for cocktails. I hate these gatherings almost as much as I hate the pretense of this relationship. I need to stand up for myself and end this situation between Nick and me before it goes any further, but he and my father are practically inseparable and the last time I tried to talk about it, he blew me off.

The wife of a state senator approaches us in her ten-thousand-dollar gown that accentuates her assets. I don't know who she is, but she's one of those women who likes you to your face and then tells everyone in private that you're a cunt. I would know because I overheard her call me that at the last event. Frankly, I couldn't care less because she's insignificant to me just like all these people in this room. "So, Claudia, your father said you're going to be working alongside Nick once you two make it official."

"Oh, I don't like discussing myself at these things," I answer. It's my usual retort because what I really want to say is there is never going to be anything between Nick and me, and if he's lucky, I'll keep his secrets. I don't tolerate Nick's touch and I haven't let him have more than a kiss.

"Always so modest, isn't she?" Nick says, smiling like the devilish snake that he is.

"If you'll excuse me, I need the ladies' room." I walk away and then grab a glass of wine on the way to the bathroom, tossing it back before setting it on a nearby empty tray.

CHAPTER ONE

CLAUDIA

I TAKE A CALMING BREATH, AND THEN I OPEN THE door to the state room where the party is just starting. The sound of the doors immediately draws attention to me, and my father smiles and walks directly toward me with power and status like he always does. His air of confidence is so strong that I don't know how to combat it, but how I wish I did.

"I'm so glad you could join us this evening, my dear," he says loudly, bending slightly to give me a kiss on my forehead. His saccharinely sweet greeting draws the adoring gaze from his many admirers, but I know it's all a show. He's furious that I'm late. His eyes meet mine with a look of disapproval.

"So am I," I answer, tilting my head in a light bow.

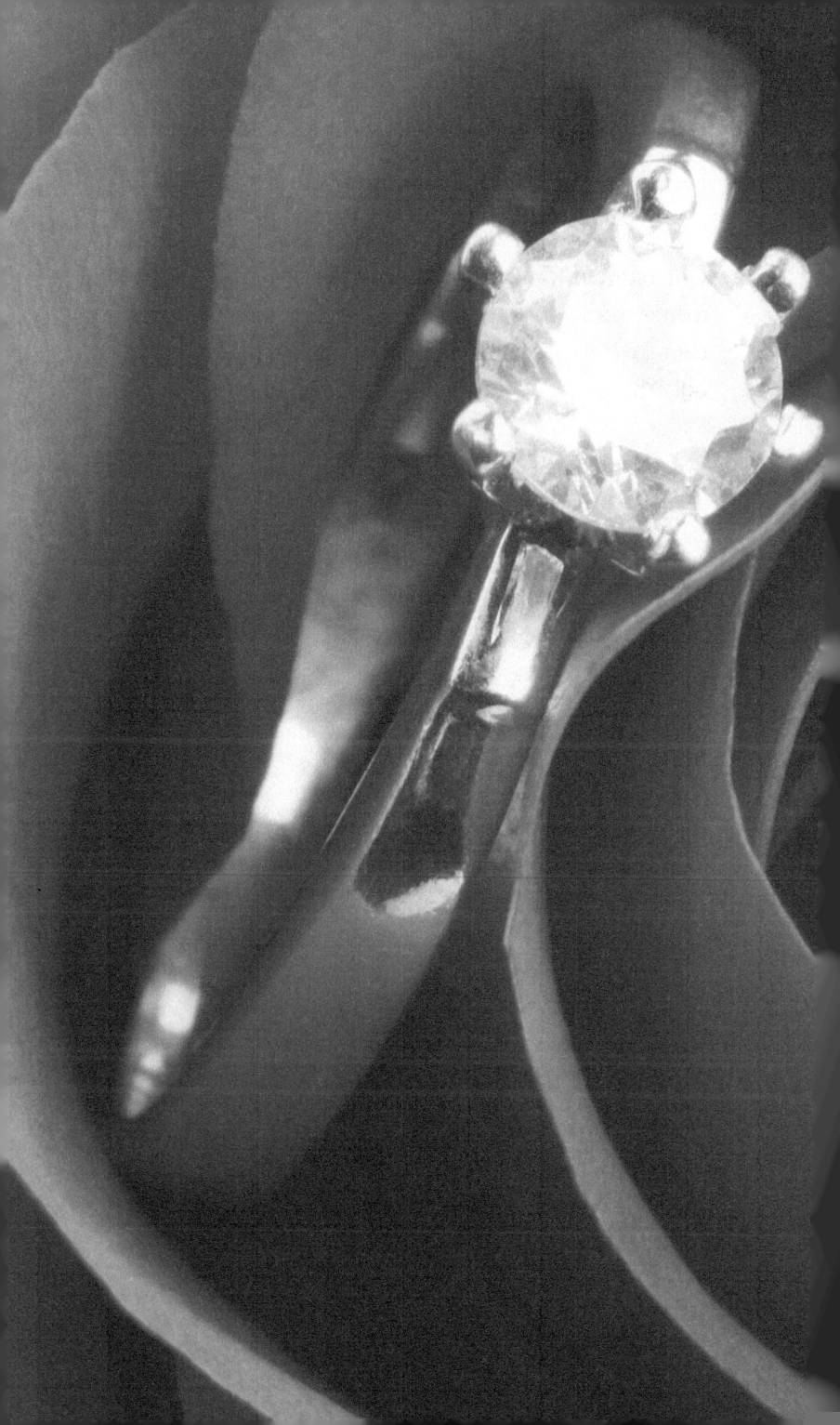

He ends the call with us, and I want to bust his head.

Ian's seething, and I see the wheels turning in Jack's head.

"Don't worry. He won't be in charge for much longer." Our old man can't be trusted by his own children, which means he's no longer capable of keeping us under his thumb. He's lost his last hold on us. My mother was the only thing that kept us strong and loyal to him.

"I'm sorry about your mother, but there are matters that still need to be handled." There is no greeting. He goes straight to his bullshit. His dismissive voice almost sends me through the phone to choke him. If any of us could be labeled a mama's boy, it was me.

"You're a heartless son of a bitch," I bark out.

"I'm sorry you feel that way, but we still have enemies and there is a problem with the Espinosa clan."

"What do you mean?" I ask. This isn't the time to worry about petty shit that our soldiers could handle while we are grieving.

"They just shot up our warehouse on Manheim." I close my eyes and take a deep breath. As much as I hate it, the bastard is right. This is something that demands a response from the family.

"What the fuck do you mean?" Ian asks.

"Did I stutter, you dumbass kid?" Ian and my father hate each other, but this has reached a new level.

If my father was standing in the same room right now, my brother would put a bullet in his head. Maybe that's why our father has such brass balls. "Who the hell are you talking to? I might be the product of your marriage, but as far as I'm concerned, I no longer answer to you. I hold you responsible for my mother's death," Ian hisses.

"Jack, get your brother in check. I already have enough to deal with. The funeral will be in three days. Clean up this mess before it gets out of hand and they think they can take over."

"We saw her last night and were supposed to head back over for our morning visit," I say, wondering how the hell this happened.

"I know, I know." Jack presses his hand to my shoulder.

"It doesn't make any sense."

"She was too damn old to be having a baby," Ian adds, slamming his glass down.

"What we need to do is give our love to our little brother, who she loved," I say. Jack was right about him, and I understand that now. She wouldn't want anything to happen to him because she loved him. She said John was a precious gift that she treasured and that we should too.

"You've had a change of heart," Jack accuses.

"Look, he's my brother, just like you two, but it's hard to bond with the little guy. We've only seen him once in the hospital. He's sick, and he's with the nurse now."

A knock interrupts our conversation. "Enter."

Jack's housekeeper, Nova, enters, frowning as she sees us. Her face is red and blotchy from her own tears shed for my mother, who everyone loved. "Mr. MacNamara, your father is on the phone for you," she says with a hiccup. My skin crawls at the mention of him. Ian's entire form Ian changed. His body tightened and his face hardened.

"Thank you." She leaves us, closing the door behind her.

We both stand around my brother's desk as he sits and answers the call on speaker. "Hello, sir."

"What about the baby?" I ask. Our mother gave birth about a week ago to a little boy, and he was the reason she'd been sick. In my opinion no woman her age should be carrying a baby. The risk is too great. Childbirth, although necessary and miraculous, is insanely brutal to a woman and my father knew it. He risked her life for another child like the selfish, arrogant prick that he is.

"You mean our baby brother?" he questions, raising his brows in that unforgiving expression of disapproval. Jack, as the eldest, took being the caretaker of us extremely seriously and that extended to the new addition. He helped raise us and I'm assuming it would be no different with our little brother now.

"Yes, of course. It's not like I forgot John is our brother. It's just—" I hate the thoughts swamping my brain, but my heart is cracked—shattered is more like it.

"If he hadn't been born, Mom would still be alive, but that shit isn't his fault, and you know it." Yes, I do. It's not his fault at all, but I'm being an irrational young man who just lost his mother. What the fuck does Jack expect?

"I expect you to act like a loving brother to an innocent child," he answers. Son of a bitch. I'm such a mess that I'm speaking my thoughts aloud. It's not something someone in my position should do no matter the circumstances. We're not the type of men who can slip up like that. I take a calming breath and attempt to gain my composure.

"Fine. All my hate will be for our father," I state, thinking about his role in this. If he hadn't knocked her up at fifty years old, she wouldn't be gone.

"I never expected anything different." Jack nodded in agreement, but dealing with the old bastard wouldn't be easy because he was still head of this family.

Jack's office door swings open. "I can't believe she's gone." Ian walks in slowly and before we can say a word, he slams his fist through Jack's wall, destroying it like it was paper. He's two years younger than me, but Ian's a muscled beast. He could rip my father's head off, and I'm betting he wants to as much as we do, but there are rules.

Ignoring the splintered wood and plaster, Jack walks over and hands Ian a glass of whiskey.

"I'm sorry," Ian apologizes, tossing back the drink as if he doesn't have busted and bloody knuckles.

"Don't be sorry, Ian. Our mother is gone, and there's nothing we can do about it. Fuck, it's killing me to consider never seeing her beautifully sweet face again," Jack says. He might be the oldest and my father's right-hand man, but that doesn't eliminate him from the pain of losing our mother. His eyes are red-rimmed as he tries to remain tough.

I pour myself a drink and toss it back in one long gulp. She'd been out of the hospital and back home for only two days before they rushed her back in.

The light music coming from the kitchen is solo from Lynyrd Skynyrd's *Freebird* and I find a hint of peace. I want to sneak into there and ask what they are doing because at least they're more down to earth than the snobs in front of me.

I feel my father's hand wrapping around my bicep. I whip my head around and see the glare in his eyes while digging his nails in for good measure. "Where are you going?" my father snarls through clenched teeth so the rest of the party can't hear his violent undertone.

"Just the little girls' room," I answer, pointing to the door mere feet away while I undo his grip from my arm. "Remember I bruise, and this dress is sleeveless."

He straightens up and his demeanor softens as he looks around to see if anyone noticed. We're nearly alone except for some of the waitstaff.

"Well, don't take too long. Nick has a special announcement he'd like to make, and you need to be by his side." I'd like to ask who he swindled or blackmailed out of a fortune, but my father wouldn't take too kindly to that and frankly, it's not who I am.

"Yes, Father. I promise I'll be right there." I step away and find the ladies' room. As I enter, I'm quickly disappointed to find Nick's ex-lover and assistant there as well. It seems she's like a permanent stalker. Over the past few months, I've seen her around and I can't stand the woman. "You're like a bad fungus that just doesn't go away," I remark as if she's the dirt under my shoes.

She stares with a murderous rage in her blue eyes. "You're the one who won't go away. Why don't you pick someone else instead of my man?" she asks. I almost feel sorry for her because she's actually upset over our relationship or whatever it is.

"I didn't pick him—he picked me. If he was your man, then why is he after me?" I asked her.

"Money, of course, and you're young," she huffs, waving her hand up and down toward my body as if she doesn't look like a playboy bunny as well. I happen to know for a fact that she does look spectacular naked. Still, that doesn't change anything and I don't have time to deal with this because I'm going to catch shit for taking too long.

"You're pathetic." I walked past her and into a stall. I don't have to use the restroom; I just want her to leave me be. Thankfully, she finally makes her exit a few seconds later.

I give it a minute before I flush the toilet and then step out to clean my hands, taking the calming breath I've been needing. I know what Nick is going to announce, or at least I think I do, and I'm afraid because there's nothing I can do to stop it. My father seems to be ready to get rid of me in one way or another, and in a way that benefits him the best.

Finally, I worked up the nerve to leave the bathroom and return to the party. "Ah, there you are." Nick says, pulling me to his side for a quick peck before releasing me.

"I'd like to get everyone's attention here, please. Thank you all for coming tonight. It's such a pleasure to see everyone's beautiful faces, and your expensive ones as well," he teases with a wink.

Everyone laughs at Nick's joke, or rather his insults to the plastic ones. I put on a gracious face even though a sinking feeling hits the pit of my stomach. "I know you all are wondering why we're here. We have time before we start hitting you up for money for reelection, which we will. But there's something else going on tonight, and it's very special as well."

I fidget in my heels, and my father gives me a look that tells me to stop acting like a five-year-old, and I snap back into proper form. For as long as I can remember, I've always been my father's little daughter who behaved. The only time I've wavered was when it came to my career. I shared my grandmother's passions and that wasn't politics. Baking has been the heart and soul of my existence.

"Claudia, my dear. Will you do me the greatest honor and become my better half?" My eyes are wide open as Nick is down on one knee. I stare down at him with my mouth open, unable to speak as he holds my hand.

"Claudia," he whispers, waiting for me to answer. My mouth closes, and I don't know what to say because I want to tell him to fuck off, but I can't make a scene in front of everyone.

"She said yes," my father says, stepping in front of us. Nick slides the ring on my finger and then brings my hand to his lips, giving it a kiss. He stands and pulls me into his arms and then presses his lips to mine, and the crowd cheers. I'm the first to pull back and keep the fake smile on my face because I must put on a show. Why would they do this to me?

"Congratulations, sweet girl," my father says boomingly, kissing my cheek before lowering his voice to a whisper. "Keep up the cheerful grin. You made the right choice." He straightens up and smiles at me and then to everyone else.

"Thank you, Daddy," I say in my own sweetly perfect voice, pretending to be a happy bride-to-be so the crowd can gush over my father and his precious child.

Several of the ladies quickly rush up to me with gushing eyes and say, "Oh my goodness. We have to see it." I put my hand out with the enthusiasm my father expects and show them the rock that Nick gave me.

"Let's cheer to the future Mr. and Mrs. Mirren," my father says. Losing attention on him, he redirected it where it belonged. Everyone raises their glasses to us with a round of cheers and congratulations. Although I must say that I wasn't bothered by the distraction because I don't want it.

"Thank you, everyone," Nick adds, sliding his arm around my waist again, pulling me close. God, my skin crawls. I want to peel his fingers off my body, but I fight the urge with every ounce of strength. He takes a drink from his flute of champagne before handing it to the waiter.

"You look delectable and smell so sweet—so good I could eat you up." I can tell he was drinking a little before he made that speech and clearly had another glass. Not enough to be drunk, but definitely enough to work up the balls to get handsy with me. He's never this forward. I hate when he tries to touch me. I've made it clear to him that I'm saving myself for marriage, or at least that's what I tell him.

"So I'd like to talk to you about joining me as one of the staffers." My head tilts like this man has lost his damn marbles.

"How many glasses in are you?"

"Come on now, Claudia. You know that bakery is a pipe dream, and I need you to be serious and at my disposal." I puff out a quiet laugh and stare at him with more disillusion than I had before. Our relationship had been orchestrated by my father, and I wanted nothing to do with it. Now, I'm here dealing with a man who wants me to give up my dream to be available to fuck.

"I know what kind of disposal you'd like me to be at, but Nick, my dream isn't to spend all day on my back. If that was the case, I wouldn't need to work at all."

"Yes, but I'm not at home all the time. I'm at the office and I have needs." I close my eyes and take a deep breath. I'm sure his assistant is around here, looking for any way to assist him in those needs.

"Now is not the time for this discussion, and I will not be blamed for any outbursts." With a polite smile I walk around him and find one of the ladies to speak with.

The party continues for another hour before more and more people leave and the soiree begins to dwindle. As I mingle, Nick finds me again, this time he's a little more sober and I notice the scent of that bitch on him. I chuckle to myself. He doesn't even have the decency to keep it in his pants with my father around. Nick's phone rings at the same time as my father's. "Excuse me, sweet girl. I need to take this call."

He steps away from the group, and one of the ladies says, "Don't worry, sweetheart. You'll get used to it, and you'll have your own life while he's working." Her eyes brows raise, but with all the treatment on her face, there's hardly any expression on her face. Still, the meaning was clear. I'll be able to have my affairs too.

"Thanks." I walk away and then pretend I'm going toward the waiter who has flutes of champagne. I take one and sneak over to where Nick is on the phone. Is he talking to his girlfriend that he thinks I'm not aware of, or is it someone else? He couldn't have been more obvious about needing sex while working.

"We have the warrant," my father walks up to him and says. Nick nods, ending his call and then dialing another number. "We need to organize the men because I want this to move smoothly before he has a chance to hide anything. Getting these fucks would make both our careers."

The calls end and my father says something that actually shocks me. "As much as I want this alliance with you and my daughter, if I catch you with that whore, disrespecting my daughter and myself, it's over."

"I swear she came onto me, but I told her to go home."

"Good. She deserves a faithful husband. I can find her one even if I lose the connections. Maybe a treasurer would be a better fit," he snarls, glaring at Nick.

"Understood, Sir."

I turn away and return to the party. It's business, and it's legitimate business to boot. They're going to be busting some piece of shit that would make the news. As happy as I am that he stuck up for me, it was still about his reputation and connections. A deal to be had at my expense.

I crashed into a wall of muscle only to meet the eyes of a handsome man I'd seen on screen several times. "Hello, Ms. Saunders. You're a beautiful treasure. It's such a shame that you're marrying the Attorney General when you could be with a man like me," actor Dennis Macklin says. He's Hollywood's leading heartthrob at the moment, and of course a little closer to me in age.

"I'm sure you have a bunch of sexy ladies beating down your door," I say, giving him a saucy smile. He's the type that loves flattery, I'm sure.

"I do, but you are a true thing of beauty. A man would start a war for you. You're the Helena of Troy." God, he's laying it on thick. There is no man who would do it, and I know he wouldn't. Between the booze and probably the line of coke he's already snorted, Mr. Macklin is seeing a different version of me. I don't have on a fraction of the makeup that the other women here do, and my gown, although expensive, is plain black.

"Sweet girl, there you are." I turn and see Nick approaching me.

I give him a subtle smile that is completely fake, but he's either blind to it, or he doesn't care because he smiles back and kisses my cheek before he walks out. Then, a moment later, my father approaches. "Sweet girl, I have some business to attend to. Unfortunately, that means I'll have to call you a car."

It's sick that they both call me that. I'm not sure when Nick started using it, but I find it completely revolting now. I don't have a daddy fetish and even if I did, it wouldn't be like that. It's more like hot daddies like Pedro Pascal or The McDreamy or McSteamy combo. Seriously, it's like Nick does everything he can to make me grossed out.

"Thank you, but I can fetch an Uber or cab home."

"You will do no such thing. I will not be embarrassed. A driver will be here to escort you to your apartment." I know there's no winning this argument, so I resign myself to his demands.

"Thank you, Father. Have a good night. Please be safe."

"I will. Congratulations, my dear." I nod and watch him leave too. I stayed for a bit longer before taking the car he had requested back to my apartment.

I'd left two lights on so someone would think there was someone home. It's a little trick I learned when it came to living alone in a big city. Still, the driver waits until I'm inside my building before pulling away.

I lean against the wall and look at the stupid, gaudy ring on my finger, wondering what the hell I'm going to do. There's no way I can marry Nick. I want to vomit just thinking about it.

A notification hits my phone just as I'm pondering my miserable situation. *Get some sleep. Big day tomorrow.*

Oh crap. I have the Fieri & MacNamara cake taste-testing tomorrow. I kick off my heels, unzip my dress, and shimmy out of it as fast as I can to get ready for bed. I was exhausted from the entire ordeal and now I had a big meeting tomorrow morning that was important.

It's a huge deal, and one that could make or break my career. Nora told me the sky's the limit on her budget, but the cake has to be made soon because her husband wants a quick wedding and she loved my images on Instagram. Frankly, I was shocked she saw them. I'm not popular, and there are so many fancy designers in the city—and she picked me, so I have to do one hell of a job for her.

I set the ring in my jewelry box, wanting to forget it even exists. Unfortunately, my father will make sure that won't happen.

Thankfully, I do have a brilliant excuse to keep it tucked away, which I am most certainly taking advantage of. Cleaning off the light makeup I put on is a must. I didn't do a bunch of it, but it's more than I normally wear on a daily basis. I wash the crap off my face and feel a bit freer before I leap onto my plush bed. Sleepy time for me. My eyes glance at the clock on the nightstand, and it's already midnight. Ugh—four hours.

Is it terrible that I hope whoever they go to arrest gives them trouble and he just happens to shoot one, or maybe both, of my problems? *Of course, it is,* I mutter to myself. That's not who I am and that's a terrible thing to consider even if they are shitty people. My father is verbally cruel, but he's never laid a hand on me and Nick is just a slimy worm. I should just stick up for myself and move on—when I grow a spine. Putting the pillow over my head, I let sleep take me for the few hours I can get.

CHAPTER TWO

CONNOR

THE ALERTS HIT MY PHONE JUST BEFORE everything went down, so I hit all the locks and hidden vaults. Then I stand and adjust my suit as if nothing is amiss. I've dealt with matters like this before. "We're about to be raided, boys. Let's welcome our guests and make sure everyone leaves here safe. We don't want any incidents." My security nods and follows me as we move to the door of my office.

The sound of music comes to a screeching halt as power is cut to the building as I expected. The pricks truly have no damn respect for the people inside the club. My men know damn well it's not a rival organization attack; no, it's a political one. From the looks of the armed fucks outside, it's the ATF and the SWAT team brought to me by the asshole governor of the state. I'm on the phone to my security when the generator kicks on, but with only the basic lights—exactly what these assholes wanted.

On the loudspeaker from outside the club, they say, "The club is closed due to violations. Please exit in an orderly fashion."

I come out of my office and address the crowd. "Calm down, everyone. The governor's a prick. Please follow his request, but remember that when you go vote next time." I look to my men and say, "He's only pissed because his mistress is fucking one of my employees."

I wink over at one of my guys who has the brunette by the waist. It's the latest *fuck you* to the governor I added. It's not my fault the asshole couldn't stay in Springfield where he belongs. We have enough crooked politicians in Chicago and don't need his shady ass here causing more trouble. He screwed up, showing his hand, and now my man Tommy was getting a blowjob from Saunders's mistress. Tommy had only tucked little Tommy into his pants when the lights came back on, and I'm not going to complain because that was the point of him coming to the club tonight. I wanted a lot of proof to give the asshole. I got it on video, and there were multiple witnesses.

"Open the door and follow them out," I address my men. I want the least amount of conflict and confrontation with these assholes. They are going to huff and puff, grandstanding like they always do and then leave with nothing. Last time this jagoff tried it, I had my lawyer right there and sent them packing before he could get through the door. Unfortunately, I wasn't forewarned today. Oh well, next time I'll be prepared.

The team of armed men wait for the people to leave before they enter with their guns. "Are those really necessary, Governor Prick Face?" I wave at all the suited-up, jacked men with their weapons aimed at my guards.

"Precaution." I smirked because he answered as addressed. It's childish, but it is still funny. I stride toward them with my own level of arrogance and my men following behind me. They level their weapons and I put my palms up as I approach so the prick doesn't freak out like the little sissy that he is. How can he be that large and be that soft?

"Do you have a warrant for this raid?" I challenge him. I'm sure he has some bullshit that he calls legal, but it won't stand up in court. It's enough to ruin my night, though. What he thinks he'll find here is a wonder to me.

His little puppet behind him waves the piece of paper with authority. "We were given a tip that you were holding women against their will in your basement storage."

"Well, if that was the case, you just let them out," I say with a chuckle, rolling my eyes at the arrogant bastard. He knows damn well there was no tip because it was just a stunt to shut down my club for the night. Of the many organizations in the city, we were one of the few that never trafficked humans.

"We don't want to frighten the patrons, but we still need to check," the attorney general says. I hate that pipsqueak freak, and I want to bury the bastard one day. Although sending him to federal prison would probably make me a lot happier.

"More like you didn't want them to stay and witness your ineptitude, or maybe you didn't want them to have a good time after you left." I direct my attention solely to the governor and say, "By the way, Suzy says hello, or she would have if her mouth wasn't so full. It was so damn hard to hear with all that dick garbling."

"What? What the fuck are you talking about?" he snarls, losing his cool. After his wife left him, his manhood had taken a serious blow, and I wanted to add another one-two punch.

"Your latest mistress just left." I wink at him and then smirk. "My men will escort you around, but I have work to do since you've just cost me money and my lawyer needs to hear about this." I snatched the warrant from his puppet's hands and read the one-page pile of horseshit. Just like I expected, the prick judge that signed off on it is his buddy. They both need a bullet to the head.

What happened between him and my piece-of-shit father? The feud has only grown over the years, and the only people to have suffered from it are my brothers and me.

"You're a prick," he says.

"Takes one to know one. And trust me—you will pay for screwing me out of five thousand dollars in revenue tonight. It's our busiest night." I slowly nodded my head because he best damn believe he's going to pay for ruining my money. I don't play with my funds.

"You can say what you want. You don't earn that much unless it's to sell drugs." He can fuck off with that bullshit. He's a fool and lucky it's already after one because I've already earned a good chunk of money. Fridays are killer for me. I make around twelve thousand for doing nothing. What he doesn't realize is that my high-end club hosts the right people who could cost him his re-election.

"Let's test your piss, Saunders, and then we'll talk about drugs, old man. I bet they let your ass skate on by with drug tests while you got powder all over your nose. Now piss off," I say, waving my hand, and turn.

"Do you want us to arrest him, sir?" I whip my head around to see who opened their dumb-ass mouth to speak. One look at him, and I want to pick a fight for fun. It would be foolish and tough, but after years of practice, I'd beat his ass.

I glare at the lead uniformed prick who looks and sounds like he 'roids up for breakfast. "For what, cunt? You're in my establishment, insulting and harassing me with a flimsy warrant. I'll be out in hours and I'll be filing a nice lawsuit." I wink at him.

Two men come down, interrupting my rant, which pisses me off. "Boss, the place is empty. There's no sign of women held captive in here." I smirk at them.

"You're all wasting your time. I don't need to hold women captive, unlike some," I remarked, giving the governor an obvious stare.

"Do another sweep and make it thorough," the governor says, sneering at me.

"That's fine. Everything here is on camera. Every single thing you and your men do is being recorded, so I hope your men are aware that I'll be ready to press charges if anything is tampered with, destroyed, or otherwise ruined."

"Is that a threat?" AG Mirren questions. The little pussy is pathetic, and I'd love to snap his neck.

"No, it's a promise. I'm aware of my rights, and my lawyer is, too." I cross my arms and smirk.

Mickey walks up to me and says, "Boss, Mr. O'Neill is on the line."

"Good. Perfect timing." He hands me the phone. "Hello, James. Please come to the club. I've received a warrant, and I've been raided by Governor Saunders and Attorney General Mirren."

"They have a warrant?" he asks.

"Yes. They have a flimsy one that's signed by one of their buddies, Judge Melendez," I explained. The guy they have in their fucking pocket. I had my sources and I was aware that Melendez was just as dirty as my brothers and I.

"I'm on my way," James answers.

"Good. I'll see you soon." I end the call and hand back the phone. "Excuse me." With a hint of arrogance, I walk around the bar and pour myself a drink without a damn care in the world because I know it's pissing them off.

"Would you care for one while you wait? Oh, and is it normal for you to serve a warrant with a hint of booze on your breath?" I asked Mirren.

"We were celebrating my engagement when the warrant was issued. Couldn't miss a perfect opportunity," Mirren said, sounding too damn smug. I wonder what dumb bitch he got to marry him. She's got to be after his money or status because he's a prick too. There's nothing special about this slender dweeb in glasses who is getting too old to be hanging on the coattails of another grown man.

"The bitch got to be dumb or after your money to settle for you."

"Watch your mouth, MacNamara," the governor says, catching me off guard. "Why are you two getting married?"

"I'm marrying—"

"It will be in the papers tomorrow. You can read it like everyone else."

"Sounds uninteresting," I sighed, taking another drink from my glass, staring at the governor over the rim.

We have a bit of a silent standoff. The fucking legal thug with his gun stares at me, trigger finger itchy. "Calm your tits there, Rambo. You aren't here to be offloading. If you come here on a non-working night, you could offload." I toss him a wink and chuckle. For a brief moment he actually looks interested.

Another ten minutes of searching finds absolutely nothing, and they're forced to leave with their tails between their legs, of course. My lawyer arrives about twenty minutes after they leave. "Sorry that I took so damn long. I was sleeping when I got the notification and call," he explains, looking nervous as he enters my club all frazzled, hair out of place.

I wave him off and raise my glass, waving it. "It's fine, James. You live thirty minutes away. I'm surprised you made it here that fast."

"Sure. I'll take a glass of whatever you got. By the way, I did break a few traffic laws, so I might get a nice ticket in the mail."

"Send me the bill. I'll add it to the other charges I'm sending the AG." Tomorrow I'll find out who the AG is marrying and then I'll find a way to ruin that shit because it obviously has something to do with the governor.

A thought comes to my mind, the mysterious daughter no one has seen in years, Claudia Marie Saunders. Rumors are that she's in an all-girl school in Switzerland. I'm not sure how old she is, but I'll have to look for a picture. She has to be around seventeen or eighteen if she's still in school. That's sick of Saunders.

A WHINY GROAN COMES FROM THE SIDE OF THE bed, and I swear it's annoying as fuck as I'm trying to sleep. I turn, and my face is licked.

"What the hell? Go away." I shoved his face back while whipping my own head against the pillow, trying to get some space and clean the slobber off me. I should have him in the other room, but I've been neglecting him lately and he's a big baby.

Still, I know it's time for me to get up and take Cain for a walk. I crawl out of bed even though I just got home only a few hours ago after dealing with some bullshit from our enemies. First I had to go to the docks in the morning and then the damn governor at the club. One damn problem after another.

Gov. Donavan Saunders is never gonna let up until we deal with him for good, but there's nothing we can do just yet. There are way too many people who know he's number one on our shit list.

He's been a thorn in our sides for longer than I can remember. We tried to play nice, but it was no dice with him. He wants all or nothing from us. My brother Jack doesn't understand that Saunders is gonna have to be put down. Jack's still holding out hope that this will end peacefully, but with a man like Saunders who feels like he's untouchable because of his rank, he's too damn stubborn for his own good; last night told me that. I must find a way to hit him where it hurts so he learns who he's fucking with.

I climb out of bed because sleep is for the dead, and then I get myself ready because there's nothing else I can do except take this beast of a dog out before he pisses on my floor. He's a well-trained animal, but there's only so much one can do when they've got to go, and Cain's getting antsy.

I rub my eyes and walk over to the bathroom to take a piss and get my day started. Fuck, I hope this doesn't turn into another shit show. I need a damn vacation with a hot broad riding my dick or something. Checking out my face, I need a shave, but it can wait because I'm tired as fuck right now. I slip on a pair of joggers and a tee shirt and then give my big boy a whistle.

"Come on, you big baby. Let's take you outside," I say, holding the bedroom door open. His paws scrape the wooden floors wildly as he makes his way through my bedroom and out into the hallway. He's trained to hunt those who would try to harm me, but the rest of the time, he's extremely chill. Tough as nails when needed, something that could be said about all of us MacNamara men—except for my father, who was always like a wild fucking chihuahua or something.

I lead him into my secured backyard so he can do his business and play for a bit while I check in on my daily numbers for the club. I have to be at Mac's around ten to make sure everything is running smoothly, but I plan to have a drink or two and unwind now that John has been found.

As shitty as yesterday was, nothing compared to when my little brother John had been taken. Maybe that's why I have no chill with the governor. Fuck him. I still wonder if he was involved in my brother's abduction. We don't know all the players involved and I'm not counting him out yet.

I'm in the middle of sending O'Neill an email about the club when my brother calls. What the fuck is he doing calling at this ungodly hour? "Fuck." Whatever he has to say can't be good at this time of the day. He's busy with John and his woman, so he doesn't call for no reason.

"What's up?" I grumble, with my throat still a little hoarse. It's so damn early the sun is barely out in the middle of summer.

"Connor, I know you're busy, but can you do me a favor and go to the bakery for me?" Did he just ask me that? A silly fucking chore like I'm an errand boy. Can't he send one of his men to pick up a cake or dessert?

"What? I'm kind of busy. I've been dealing with the shit you've been letting slide over the past three weeks." While he's been raising our little brother and playing kissy face with his bride-to-be, I've had to endure the brunt of the business, meaning no fucking sleep and crazy-as-hell problems.

I've managed to get everything under control, even after last night's bullshit with the governor. That prick was probably pissed because his latest mistress was sucking some other guy's dick in our club. Not my fucking problem that he can't keep his whores in their place. Hell, he can't even keep his wife in line. She left his ass years ago.

"I'm sorry, but something has come up and Nora will be upset if I ruin the baker appointment. Apparently, she's super famous, and she made this fabulous cake that caught Nora's eye while I left her trapped in the house." Oh, this isn't just a treat. This is for the big-ass wedding cake. A thought comes to mind, and I picture the bride and groom topper. I should have them put a leprechaun on there because Jack's a lucky bastard that Nora would marry his old ass.

Nora's a sweet woman who did an amazing thing last year by raising John and helping him grow in a way none of us could have imagined. "Is she still pissed about you going out of town?" I chuckled, enjoying his misery because we had to do the babysitting. I actually like Nora, but it is fun busting my brother's chops.

"No. I made it up to her several times." I can just picture the jerk grinning on the other end of the phone because he's getting off all the time, while I'm too tired to even get my hand on my dick let alone find someone to get off with.

"Lucky fucker," I grumble.

"Damn right, I am. I want to have a word or two with her family today." Instantly, my body stiffens, and I'm out of my playful mood. Who knows what arrangement they had with my father for Nora's hand, and they aren't happy that Jack and Nora fell in love and they get nothing. I've never liked the Fieris, and for good reason. They're our enemies.

"You sure you don't want backup?" I don't like the idea of Jack being around her father. He's a piece of shit, just like ours. I still haven't acquitted our father of the kidnapping of my brother. Even if all the evidence points to Espinosa, I can't shake the feeling that my father was involved. And Fieri's no better. He wanted to pawn his daughter off on us years ago. He forced Nora to flee instead of letting her live her own life.

"I'm taking Ian with me for this one." Good. Ian is nuts and always ready to work.

"That's what I was going to suggest. There's no damn way I'm in the mood for it. I'm already tired."

"Too much partying?" I fucking wish that was the problem. Having fun hasn't been part of my vocabulary in years, thanks to my father and the loss of my mother. My hands are in too many pots to be relaxed enough to enjoy the good life.

"No, I had a run-in with that dickhead governor," I grunt.

"And you didn't tell me?" he snarls. I should have called him after they showed up, but for as much as I bitch, he needs peace.

"You're in your own happy little world and have enough on your plate. Besides, I'm a big boy. Dad hates that prick and keeps picking fights with him, so Saunders's people pulled a raid on the club last night and had it shut down for no reason. I was able to get it taken care of, but it cost us closer to ten grand than the five I thought it would. I'm going to sue them, but it will probably cost as much as we lost in just the legal fees alone." It's more about principle than anything.

"That prick knows what he's doing. We need to have a talk with Dad again and tell him to quit it with the asshole. The war has to end because it serves no purpose. Two old bastards going head-to-head, and the only ones paying for it are us." They need to fight it out. It would be a pathetic match because they are both out of shape and old.

"So damn true. Send me the address, and I'll take care of it," I tell him. Enough with the heavy talk. I have too much to do today and I'm fucking beat. Besides, I'm holding back the bigger bit. Mirren is getting married and the governor is invested in the situation somehow.

"I owe you one, Connor."

"That you do, but I'm not doing it for you. I'm doing it for my favorite sister-in-law. I owe her," I say, knowing he's going to ask questions. The smile on my face grows, and I look up at the camera for my backyard just in case he can see me. He has access to all of the cameras on the family compound.

"Why do you owe her?" Jack asks, his jealousy on full display. I wish I could see his face. My grin was a mile wide at the moment even though my dog was tearing up the grass.

"You're not an asshole anymore," I chuckle, enjoying my own little petty torments.

"Fuck off."

"You know...maybe I don't owe her." I'm sure he wishes he was in front of me right now so he could deck me one, but he's not, so he'll have to settle for getting all red in the face. As kids and young men, we enjoyed taking our frustrations and training out on each other, sparring and wrestling until we were too damn sore to move. It worked to make us strong and tough enough to deal with the hard times. Our bond as siblings is unshakeable, so despite being exhausted, I still plan on running the errand for him, or rather, for Nora.

"Just do it for us," Jack snarls, getting worked up, which amuses me so damn much. That's what the asshole gets for working me to the bone lately.

I find amusement in his aggravation as I end the call. I'm happy for my brother, even if I like to tease him. It's part of my job as his brother and he knows it, even if he doesn't like it.

"Come on, Cain." He looks up from his spot where he's digging a nice hole. "Time to go in. Paws," I tell him as we reach the pad by the door. He wipes his feet before coming in so his ass doesn't track mud everywhere. I walk into the kitchen and speak with my housekeeper. "Good morning, Anna."

"Good morning, Mr. MacNamara. I have Cain's food ready, and your coffee has just finished." She has worked for me over the past four years. I think she's in her late twenties, but I haven't asked because it's not my business. My father always told us to keep our female employees at arm's length because they could get the idea that we want more than just their paid services, which I was sure to be true for some. I wouldn't know personally because I've always kept to that policy.

"Thank you. I will be leaving shortly, so I will need just a bagel to go," I say while scrolling through my messages because my day never ends. Running our operations isn't just about busting heads and selling weapons, so our daily lives require working hard as hell. Shit, we just invested in a major building complex for the city which will bring a lot of money to the lakefront.

"Yes, sir." She prepares it with an eager smile, which is unneeded, but I suppose if she frowned, I'd probably start worrying about my meals and even my life.

I quickly slip on a nice light gray suit with a pink tie, so I look like I belong in the place. It's a quaint shop in the Northside of the city that probably costs a fortune to rent, so the cakes must be amazing and expensive. Not that I care, but it's what Nora wants, so it's what she'll get. There isn't anything Jack won't do for her, which includes making me her errand boy.

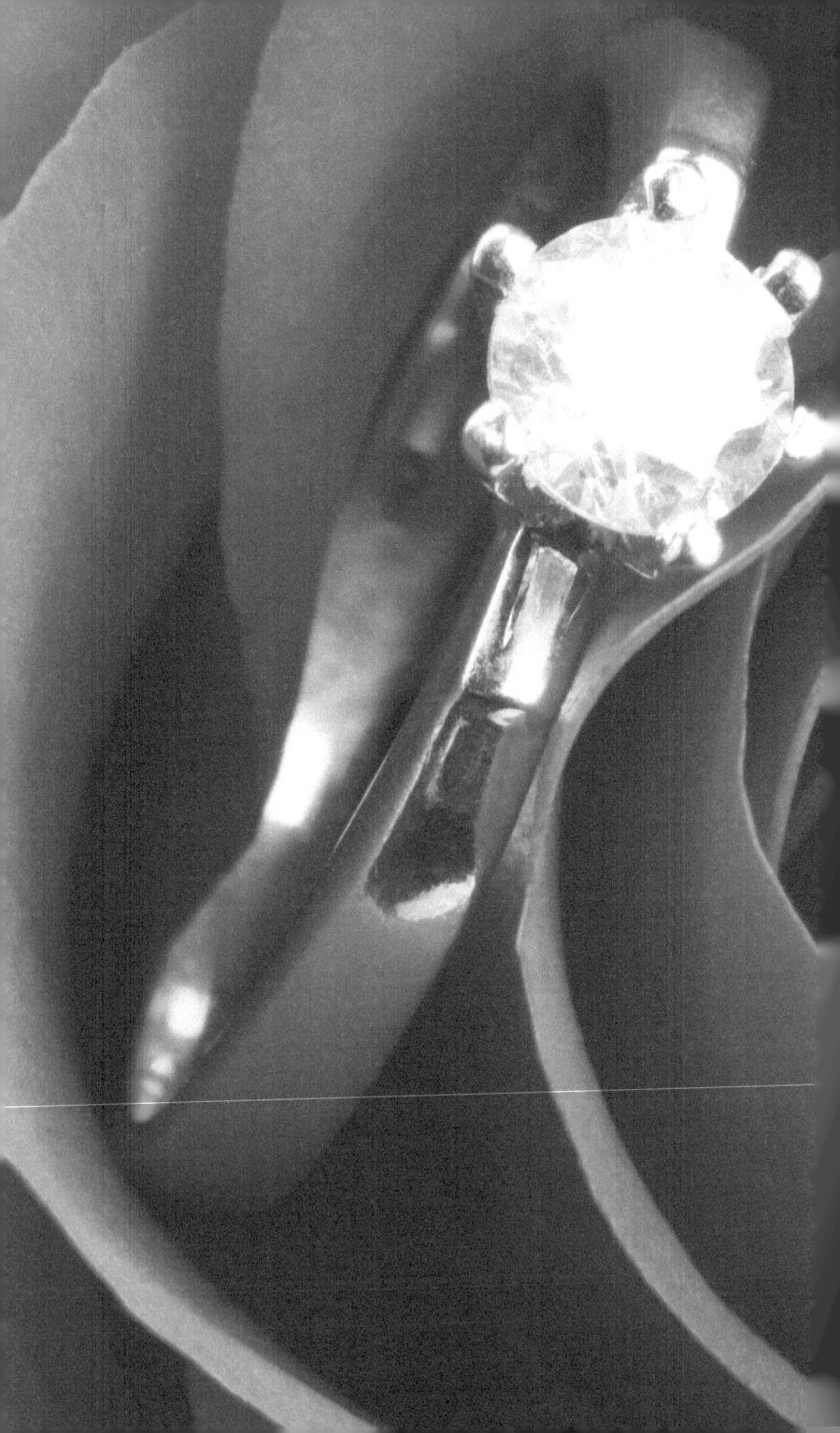

CHAPTER THREE

CLAUDIA

I STRETCH MY ARMS AND LET OUT A HAPPY SIGH. Today is my first big cake presentation, and I'm so excited. I've been baking for a lot of smaller clients and filling orders for birthday parties at my bakery, but this one is for a large wedding for a billionaire. They're coming into my shop after checking out my Instagram account. I've done so many cake designs online for displays and presentations.

I've spent the past two days picking out designs. If I didn't have my father harassing me to attend last night, I would still be perfecting my ideas for this tasting. There is a lot riding on this. Most of my designs are just for show. Nora is my make-or-break moment.

She seems like a sweet woman, so I'm not so afraid of the whole Bridezilla thing. Nora is so insanely pleased with my work that she asked for something similar to the ones online, but today is a taste test to pick flavors and colors. I'm actually looking forward to meeting her. Her husband, not so much. He's been rumored to be a bad man—Jack MacNamara. I might not know everything my father deals with in his daily affairs as the Governor of Illinois, but I'm well aware of his pleasure in bringing down the MacNamara family.

"Oh my God." Please tell me that's not who he raided last night. I check my messages, and there's nothing from Nora. I take a deep breath and decide to carry on as usual.

It's only five in the morning and the sun still has a while before making its appearance, but I have to get to work. Slipping out of the covers, I slid into my slippers next to the bed and walked into the bathroom. It's going to be a busy but happy day. I refuse to believe otherwise. As the daughter of an authoritarian father, I've learned to live my life with pure optimism and let everything else wash off me.

After using the restroom, I turn on the sink and I'm reminded of the rock that was on my finger. Ugh. "Take a calming breath." Engaged. I'm engaged. Last night had been an evening I want to forget, but of course, I accepted because that's the good girl I am—always doing my father's bidding, especially since my mother ran off with another man.

I remembered Nick Mirren asking for my hand at the party with my father as if it was nothing. Freezing, unable to respond, my father answered for me. Nick slid the ring on my finger without giving me a chance to refuse and then kissed me in front of everyone. The memory so vivid and still so revolting.

We've never been intimate because I have set boundaries, not the other way around. If he had his way, I would have been spread out on his office desk like I found him with his secretary the first time we met two years ago. Of course, I was completely turned off, and she was summarily dismissed a week later. My father then began making it his priority to push the newly appointed Attorney General in my face. Nick is too old for me. I'm twenty years old, and he's like thirty-four. Eww. So gross.

I should call it off, but my father would be so disappointed in me. He's already so disappointed that I took a different path from political science because he wanted me to be his campaign manager, but my love for baking has always been in my heart. Worse yet, it had been my paternal grandmother's love. She'd left me the money for the shop that I opened below my apartment. He doesn't understand it, and I believe that's why he's pushing my marriage with Nick so hard. It's his hope that he can make me change and join the fold one way or another.

However, no matter how many times I stood alongside my father at major political events, my soul ached with the need to become a baker so much that I entered a program and gained a degree as a pastry chef in only eighteen months. I haven't been seen in public in three years until last night, so I hope it doesn't make the papers or anything. I told my father that I didn't want to be part of the political circus.

Six months ago, I opened up Claudia's Cakes, and I use my paternal grandmother's maiden name so that no one connects me to my father. I want to stand on my own two feet, branding my desserts my way. So far no one has made the connection, and I'd like to keep it that way for as long as possible. Although, once the engagement is announced, I believe the cover will be blown.

Hopefully I'll be able to maintain my career with Nick working all the time. Until then, I'll be working and keeping my ring hidden in my jewelry box because it doesn't belong in the kitchen, anyway. At least, that's what I tell myself.

After a quick shower, I pin up my hair and dress professionally. There's a great deal to do before my appointment with Nora and Mr. MacNamara, which is at ten. That gives me plenty of time to make treats to display after they leave.

I exit my apartment upstairs before the sun rises, locking the door behind me before taking the stairway down that leads to the back room of my bakery. When I unlock the door, the fresh smells of chocolate, vanilla, and sugar hit me. Right now, I don't have the money to hire any employees so my bakery hours are from noon to four, but once I do, this place will hopefully open early and there will be the smell of fresh pastries in the air.

I step into the storefront and take a look at my window displays. I need to make some changes to what I put on display today. I love the pastel look, but summer is here, so we need to toss out the spring colors, and I want everyone to feel the beachy vibes. Soon fall will be around the corner, so I need to make a template for that.

My heart jumps as I consider the variety of cookies and treats that I can bake for the Christmas holiday season. Taking a deep breath, I inhale the imaginary smell of cinnamon and mint of Christmas and then decide to make a couple of notes before getting to work. I'm totally getting way ahead of myself, but I can't help it.

Digging into the large walk-in cooler, I pull out the rack and ice the cakes I have for a party coming up and then slide them back inside, marking off the order. It's nearly time, when a message comes in from my father. *Call Me Now.*

I wash my hands quickly and call him back because I don't have time for this. "Daddy, I don't have a lot of time. I'm about to meet a client about a wedding cake order," I inform him. He forgets that he's not the only one who is busy.

He just ignores me and talks over me. "I want to make the announcement tomorrow at a press conference." Shit. It's not something I'm prepared for.

I gather my nerve and say, "Daddy, I don't think that's a good idea." I was glad he hadn't shared the news already, but still, I hadn't wanted it out there yet.

"You think we need to announce it sooner?" he says. "I held it off today because I had some setbacks with my business last night, but I hoped to make your announcement a big deal."

Taking a deep breath, I confess the truth. "No. I'm not ready to marry him."

"Then why did you say yes?" he barks.

"I didn't. You said yes for me in front of everyone before I could respond," I argue.

"You're going to marry him. You will not embarrass me like your mother did, Claudia. I already let you get away with this silly baking thing that's proving to be a money drain." I want to prove him wrong, but I'm not technically rolling in the dough financially. I'm teetering on the line between red and black, but most new businesses don't make it out of the red for a long time.

"It's not fair. I shouldn't have let the farce carry on between Nick and I."

"No, you shouldn't have, but since you did, you will follow through. Enough said. Be a good girl like you're supposed to, Claudia." That was all that needed to be said because there would be hell to pay otherwise. I'm sure he could find a way to sabotage my business and that scared me a lot.

"Yes, Daddy," I said to no one since he hung up on me. I set the phone down, wanting to cry. His dismissal feels like a deep blow to the chest, as if the wind just got knocked out of me. Sometimes I wish I had the courage to speak my mind and move on from him, cutting the only family member I have left out of my life, but it's as if I can't break through that last vestige of a familial bond. Maybe one day I'll have the strength, but today isn't that day.

Wiping away the warm wetness from my face, I hear the alarm go off on my phone, alerting me that it's time for my clients to be arriving any minute now. I set up the taste-testing samples, and then I go in the bathroom to look over my appearance.

Even though I've been baking all morning, that doesn't mean I shouldn't present my best self to them. I yank off the hair net and give my amber waves a brush out before setting them up into a high ponytail. Grabbing a lint roller, I run it over my clothes. My top screams creative professional, so I hope they don't take me too lightly—but I suppose they're here for my cakes and Nora's a sweetheart, so there should be less pressure.

I take a deep breath and remember that I'm a baker, not a model or an office professional. My light pink kitten sweater and black leggings with white gym shoes should be just fine. I give myself one more look in the mirror before stepping out of the bathroom.

Just then, there is a knock at the door. It's a man in a suit, but the sunlight is beaming in so I can't see who it is. My guess is that it's Mr. MacNamara. I open the door and I'm floored—inappropriately so.

"I'm here for the taste testing." His voice is deep, strong, and clearly annoyed as he enters.

"Please come in, Mr. MacNamara." I look around him and see that he's alone.

"Thank you," he says, stepping inside my shop, making it feel so much smaller. He's built and tall, but that's not the only reason his presence owns the space. It's the way he carries himself. It's no wonder Nora is head over heels for this man. Why the hell am I seriously jealous of her?

"Where is Nora?" I ask, closing the door behind him and locking it.

"She couldn't make it. I thought she contacted you already," he says. My mouth falls open, and I'm distraught. This whole thing is pointless. I check my phone, and I do have a missed call and a voicemail. It must have come in while I was in the kitchen trying to ignore my father's calls.

CHAPTER FOUR

CONNOR

FUCK. I THOUGHT MY EYES WERE DECEIVING ME from outside, but she's got to be the most beautiful woman I've ever seen, and she's not even wearing a lot of makeup. Who the hell let her walk around looking so damn beautiful and talented?

I watched her from the window long before she realized I was there. Hell, I don't know if this place has exterior cameras, but I arrived earlier than the scheduled appointment and saw the door was closed. Scoping it out, I damn near thought of all the reasons to kidnap her ass even though I was only here for the cake—and she had a nice piece of cake.

She wasn't open for another two hours. This is a special meeting they scheduled, and I'm the lucky fuck to be getting her all to myself. My dick is so damn hard I could cut the glass in front of me, but I need to go inside before

I freak her out. I grab the door handle and feel like I could tear it off in a heartbeat. It's locked like it should be, so I knock, waiting for her sexy ass to allow me to enter.

She opens the door and her mouth falls open, but then she quickly masks the lustful attraction. I take a cool, calming breath and enter the shop. I know why when she asks for my sister-in-law. She's made the assumption that I'm Jack. The naughty girl doesn't want to upset her client.

"Good morning," I say, giving her a crooked smile with my hand out to her. She blushes and remembers her manners, sticking out her delicate hand. I take it and caress it gently.

"Good morning, sir." God, the soft, delicate feel of her skin on mine shoots up my spine, but I do my best to ignore the instant arousal. I'm here on business. Perhaps I'll take her business card and call her for a date another time.

"I'm here for the MacNamara appointment," I say, cocking my brow while keeping her hand still tightly locked with mine.

She quickly yanks it away and wipes our connection off on her pants. Fuck. Why does it make me harder? *Deny all you want, beautiful.* That refusal may actually make me want her more. "Where is Nora?"

"She couldn't make it. I thought she contacted you already," I informed her. She looks for her phone under the counter and sees missed calls.

"Oh, yes. You must be Mr. Jack MacNamara."

"Actually, he couldn't make it either. I'm Connor, his brother." I quickly correct that misguided notion so that she and I aren't on different pages. Is that why she pulled away from me?

"Oh, sorry, I thought you were…because of the wedding plans, and this is a big deal to them." That sexy blush that covered her pale cheeks is back, staining them red. It clashes with her pink kitten sweater, but I wouldn't be offended if she removed it. Damn, my mind is rushing to places it shouldn't. My brother trusted me with an important task. I can't just bend the cake designer over and fuck this whole thing up because she's got me rock hard.

"Well, they trust me to do a good job." I lean in and brush my hand over her heated cheek. I was right; she's either got the best makeup money can buy, or she's not wearing any on her delicate skin. "Are you a little warm?" I ask.

"I've been baking all morning. Sorry," she says, testing the heat of her cheek. It's a mix of the truth and a lie at the same time. I love it. Don't be too vulnerable with me because I'll take advantage of it, sweetheart.

"In that case, why don't we get this cake thing started, Miss…" I want all her details directly from her sugary-sweet, glossy pink lips. I wanted to hear everything she had to say and after we finished with the cake bullshit, maybe I'll find a reason to keep her talking.

"Claudia Murphy," she answers. She bites her bottom lip like it's a secret or something.

"Well, Claudia, please." I wave my hand, and she walks past me, giving me a perfect view of her heart-shaped ass, and I swear she adds an extra sway to her walk.

Fuck. I bite down on my knuckles, wanting it to be her ass. Wow—I'm about to grip those cheeks like a sick fucking pervert if she gives me a hint of an invitation. I'd pin her against that glass and stuff her full of my own damn cream.

"So, Mr. MacNamara." She's nervous. I'm not sure if it's the situation or me. Perhaps it's both, but I understand the shift in emotions. Although I'm not nervous, I'm feeling something.

"Call me Connor," I insist, crowding her space.

"Connor, we have several varieties of flavors. Nora didn't have a favorite because she wanted to taste them, and she said something about pleasing John? I'm assuming she meant 'Jack' in her text. Autocorrect, you know." She giggles, and normally that would annoy me about a woman, but from her it's sexy.

I shake my head and correct her assumption. "No, she means John. He's my younger brother and he has autism, so she wants to get a flavor he'll like."

She presses her hand to her lips in embarrassment. "Oh. Do you know his favorite flavor?"

"I haven't found one he doesn't like. He's a cake king." The little guy is finding it to be one of his favorite treats. Although he has been limited because it's too much sugar and he's already more than a handful at the best of times.

She leads me to the first group of slices and they scream professionally decorated and cut, but I'm not looking forward to this. I hate cake. I'll do this for Nora and Jack, and for some reason I want to see the smile on Claudia's face as well. If she's happy with someone liking her desserts, then sign me the fuck up.

I'm about to take the first forkful when I catch a glimpse of movement from the corner of my eye and see the glint of metal shining through the sunlight. The fork falls from my hand, and I leap over the counter while shots ring out and the bullets bust through the glass. I have her on the ground in seconds. She screams as the bullets whiz in the air, landing all around us and hitting the glass cases. "Stay down," I tell her.

Immediately I pull out my gun, taking aim at the vehicle outside, and get a few rounds off while I keep her down. I can feel her body shaking as she clings to me, but my mind is in fight mode. Fuck. This can't be happening right now. They're all going to die and pay for what they've done.

Who the fuck knew I was going to be here? I can't imagine my sister-in-law would have done this. My brother wouldn't even consider something like this, and once he learns of it, all hell is about to break loose.

A break in the firing gives me my chance and I take it, running outside only to see them getting back in their vehicle, so I fire away as the car speeds off. There's nothing I can do but tuck my gun back inside my specialized holster in my waistband. Fuck. There is no way to see their plates or anything right now.

Claudia is still ducked under the front counter, which thankfully is made of a sturdier frame. "It's over," I tell her now ghostly pale face, caressing it softly.

I drag her to the back room just as I notice that she's bleeding. "Fuck, let me see." I hope it's just a cut from the glass, but from the bleeding, I know she's been shot. This is all my fault and I'm going to hunt those bastards down for this.

She pushes me away, shaking her head. "No. Leave me alone. Just please leave," she sobs. Despite her protests I'm not going to let her push me away.

The sirens blare behind us as the police approach. I'm allowed to carry my firearm, so I'm not worried about it, but that doesn't mean this isn't going to start some shit. I'm going to have to deal with the police—not that I don't have them on my payroll, but where I'm at might cause a problem. None of that matters, though, because she needs a fucking doctor right now. I grab a towel nearby and press it to her arm where blood seeps down.

I walk away from her and pace, watching the front door. I pull out my phone and call my brother immediately. "It was a motherfucking setup," I snarled like a damn caged tiger ready to attack. My past few days have been one shit show after another and now this has happened.

"I'm on my way," Jack grunted. "Other than Nora and myself, the only one that knew we were coming was her. Do you think she was in on it?" he questioned. My eyes had darted toward her direction and I knew it wasn't the case.

"She's been hit, though," I inform him. That information makes all the difference. It isn't like she dipped off to the back and was able to hide before the shots went off. No, she was completely in the line of fire, getting blasted in the arm. She could have been killed and that does something twisted to my insides. It's hard to explain how pissed I am. It's one thing for someone to come after me, but to come after someone so innocent doesn't make any sense.

"What? Is she okay?" I don't like his immediate concern for her. It irritates me, and I'm irritated by that irritation. There's no way I'm jealous. Yes, she's cute and I'd like to bend her over, but that's it. Besides, Jack's getting married and in love with Nora.

"She was hit in the arm. It would have been worse if I hadn't taken her to the ground. Still, she wants me to get the fuck out of here. I can't do that. The police are on their way," I explained.

"If I were you, I would just go. Let her be taken care of by them. We don't need that drama right now, and then we can find out who came after you without the police interference." Even if he has a point, the thought of leaving her before she'd been cared for was out of the fucking question.

"Do I look like I run from bullshit?" I end bullshit one way or another, and there's no way I won't take care of this matter personally. The room seemed to grow hotter as the morning heat kicked up. It didn't help that there wasn't a front window anymore which meant the AC was useless right now. I tug at my collar, feeling the heat.

"No, but do you really want them pressing you?" No. My eyes scan for trouble while looking around for Claudia.

"I want to know more. I need to see if there are cameras. Someone waited for the perfect moment to strike," I tell him. They struck at me when I was vulnerable and when they believed my guard was down. It was almost a perfect moment and if I'd been smarter, I would have come with backup and a driver, but I didn't, especially after last night.

"I'm on my way either way, so let's get this taken care of." I had no doubt my brother would back me up. Hell, he'd barge right in if I asked.

"Hold back until the police leave, unless I need the backup." They could see his arrival as a threat and we didn't want the added drama.

"I'll keep an eye on the bakery," he adds.

"Thanks."

I walk back over to my wounded little bird and see that she's glaring at me. "This is all your fault," she hisses, puffing her ample chest out at me while her hand pressed to her wounded arm.

My eyes narrow because the pretty little thing was quick to blame this on me. "Sorry, beautiful, but there shouldn't have been anyone aware that we had an appointment today, so if it's anyone's fault, it would be yours. Who do you work for?" I demanded to know, slipping my hand around to the back of her neck and holding her tightly.

"Myself?" She goes to point to the front window, but the glass is now shattered and tears come from her eyes. "It did have my name on it." She chokes out a heart-breaking sob that actually makes my chest hurt.

If she's truly innocent, that means someone followed me or happened to just have a lucky day and spot me out on my own and decide to take their chances. I was outside lurking for way too long, leaving myself exposed without paying attention to anything but the sexy little baker. It was a momentary slip-up because I'm on alert all the time —now more than ever. "I'm sorry."

"It's okay, I suppose. I do have insurance on this place, but I'm not sure gun violence is covered." As she says that, two police cars arrive along with an ambulance and a firetruck—standard procedure.

"With this city, it probably needs an extra rider," I teased, causing her to crack the faintest of a smile.

"Chicago Police Department. We're responding to a shooting," an officer says, arriving with his gun out, pointing toward us. A second officer has his six as they approach us.

I glare at the fucks with my palms up briefly just to explain, "No shit. She needs a doctor. She's been shot, and the shooters already fled." I move to lead her to them, but they pull a gun out on me. "Stay back, sir."

I realize they can see my weapon. "Calm down," I say. "We were attacked. I need her examined, and then I can give you my report so I can leave."

"We'll need your name while you lay your weapon on the ground." I do as they say because I don't want any trigger-happy bitch acting up and accidentally shooting me. Meanwhile, the paramedics lead Claudia to the ambulance and begin to work on her arm from the back of the vehicle.

"Well, if it's not trouble himself." I recognize the cop approaching me. Antony Philomeno smirks and extends his hand while giving me a shake of his head. "Connor MacNamara. I didn't expect to see you over here and getting this young lady mixed up in anything shady." My eyes move toward her. Fuck. They seem to gravitate toward hers involuntarily. Does he want her too? I'm sure he does, but that's tough shit because I'm not going to let that happen.

I see her looking our way, and I wonder if she's able to hear our conversation. "Who says this has anything to do with me? The little baker was the one shot, and I wasn't even supposed to be here. I came here as a last-minute change of plans for my future sister-in-law. Maybe the bullet was meant for her," I say, tilting my head toward the gorgeous baker. With each word out of my mouth, her eyes turn to round saucers and her mouth widens, so it's clear the sexy little thing can hear every syllable.

"Yes, that is interesting. That's a possibility with her father's position," he says. "As the governor's kid, you have to have a target on your back. She should have a security detail. I'm surprised he doesn't have one on her even just because she's freaking a beautiful woman."

I could feel the color drain from my face before it returned to beet red with fury. "Did I hear you correctly? Claudia Murphy is the governor's daughter?" That can't be correct because I was only aware of one daughter who is around eighteen who should be in Switzerland. My eyes narrow as I lift my head toward the woman sitting in the back of the ambulance. She's Saunders's daughter? My muscles constrict, tightening with rage, blood boiling with pure anger.

"Are you telling me you didn't know that, Mr. MacNamara?" he scoffs, tilting his chin downward. He acts like he doesn't believe me, but I can't believe that we weren't made aware of it. We need to up our connections and our intel. Yes, we had some internal issues that caused disruptions. Giles had been one of those issues.

"I am. She told me her name was Claudia Murphy. All intel on that prick Saunders has his daughter as Claudia Saunders, barely eighteen, and there are no new photos anywhere. According to my sister-in-law, Nora saw Ms. Murphy's bakery videos on social media. That's the only reason I'm here as I'd rather be sleeping right now instead of running errands. I don't even like sweets, and I hate cake."

The cute little baker huffs on the last little bit as if it's an insult that I'm not a fan of sugar. I'd lick some fucking frosting off her cleavage, but that doesn't mean I care for it regularly.

Of all the women to find hot as fuck and to be completely irresistible, it has to be her. She is *his* daughter. The piece of shit who has been trying to ruin me for over the past year. All of this smells funky, and fucked up.

As much as I want to get my ass out of here, something about the situation demands that I stay. Maybe it's the fact that she was shot when it's obvious the bullet was meant for me. Fuck, those pricks are going to have hell to pay when they realize they screwed up and hit their boss's daughter instead.

Some shit isn't adding up one damn bit. We really have been set up. How did Nora find this woman and pick her out of the hundreds of bakeries in the city?

I have a million questions, but right now I'm going to get the answers with the cops around. No, all my answers are going to wait until the other side of the law is able to play.

"What questions do you have for me? I have to get out of here." I'm growing more and more antsy by the second and it all has to do with the mini lying Saunders.

"Tell me what went down in the bakery."

"I came for a cake tasting. I was about to take a bite when I noticed someone standing outside the bakery and just as I did, they opened fire. I pushed her to the ground, but I wasn't fast enough. She'd been shot, and when I had a moment, I opened fire long enough to send them running. They took off, but not before they did all this."

"Did you get a look at them?"

"No. Unfortunately my head was ducked down trying to keep it on my neck."

He looks as if I'm bullshitting him, but I honestly didn't, which pisses me off. If it wasn't for me trying to protect her, I would have gotten a look at the asshole for sure. "You aren't trying to bullshit me so you can seek your own vengeance, are you?"

"No, because I don't need to do that. Whoever this was, if they were after me, they were just hired guns. The real bastard pulling the strings would get away with it. I can't go around hunting people. I have a club to run, a family to help, and a dog to take care of. Do you understand the amount of work on my plate?" I say, adjusting my now blood-stained cuffs and checking my expensive watch as if I'm annoyed with his insinuation.

"You're a great liar, MacNamara, but remember—we'll be keeping an eye on you." I roll my eyes at the cop trying to do his job, knowing that he's not going to do shit because they try to stay out of these matters.

"I don't care. Go ahead because you're not going to find anything. My gun is legal, and my actions were in self-defense today," I remind him. I have a conceal and carry and make sure everything I do is above board when I deal with the police—at least when I want them to see me.

"Keep your actions clean, and we're good." He gives me a stern look, admonishing me, but he doesn't believe a word I'm saying. I don't answer to him so I don't care what he believes.

"I will. Now—if there are no more questions, I need to check on the baker. My sister-in-law is still without a wedding cake, and she's going to be pissed at me. You know how bridezillas can be. She won't care if we were both shot." I wink at him and walk away. Nora will probably cry when she finds out what happened, but these assholes don't need to know it. She has a heart of gold unlike the devil spawn of Saunders.

I walk up to the fucking lying cunt in the back of the ambulance. "Well, hello, Miss Saunders. It seems you lied, and I saved your life for nothing. Is that why you wanted me to leave before I found out about your fucking secret? Were the cakes poisoned?"

She whips her head back as if I slapped her. "I would never poison anyone."

"But you set me up."

"You're nuts. I didn't do anything, and I didn't tell anyone that you were coming to the bakery. Hell, I didn't know you'd be there."

"No." I grab her by the throat, and I'm so close to her that it seems so intimate, like we're about to kiss. "You were going to let someone kill my brother and my sweet innocent sister-in-law."

"I wouldn't," she stammers, but she doesn't fight me. I'm not sure if she's afraid or that fucking submissive. I hate that both concepts turn me on.

"Don't fucking lie. You're scum, just like your father, and I'd watch your back if I were you. The second I have proof, I'll forget that I had any sympathy or desire for you." I push my hand off her throat and storm away from the ambulance.

I walk up the street with a steel spine, holding my head high and my temper back, and call my brother. "Pick me up on the corner."

"Already here." He pulls up, and I hop inside.

"What the hell was that about?" he asks as I close the door.

I scrub my hand over my face and shake my head. "She's the fucking governor's daughter."

"You have to be fucking kidding me. That doesn't make any sense. We didn't get that when we scoped her out."

"I wish I was."

We're both silent for about six blocks when I say, "We need someone to hack Nora's phone."

"Don't you dare accuse my wife."

"She's not your wife yet, and I'm not accusing her of shit. I'm thinking someone had to lead her to that fucking bakery. Someone had to know. As much as I want to believe Claudia was involved in the shooting, it doesn't make sense that she'd risk getting shot in the process."

"Yeah, she was a sitting fucking duck, so something doesn't add up. Do you think it's the governor, or an enemy of both of ours?"

At once, we both blurted out, "Espinosa." We hadn't nabbed the fucker yet, so there was a chance that he could be the one.

"He's on the run and he's gotten to us from the inside before, so it's possible." We pop onto the expressway, and fear worries in my brain. If she's not the enemy, she's in danger and I left her as an open target. I don't say shit because we're just thinking out loud, and she could be just as corrupt as her father but with a gorgeous face and perfect ass.

"We'll have to figure it out. For now, I want to get home, shower, and then get some sleep. I'm tired and pissed off." My body aches and I'm feeling the weight of the past thirty-six hours.

"I'll have one of the guys get your vehicle after we run cursory surveillance and look for cameras from a six-block radius. After the shit with John, I'm a little more cautious, so I've already dispatched a team to hit the areas around the perimeter and to move inward as the cops leave."

"Good." He stops in my driveway, and I exit his ride. "Take it easy, and tell Nora I'm sorry about the cake."

"Trust me when I say that will be the least of her concerns when she learns that you were shot at."

When I get through my front door, my dog is anxious to see me and jumps all over my chest. "Fuck," I groan. "Okay. Let's go for a walk." I take him around the estate briefly before going back to the house and settling down on my bed for a long damn nap. The club will be calling me tonight to monitor it, so as much as I hate doing it, I have to go in. I set my alarm and get back to business as usual all the while thoughts of the pretty baker linger in my head.

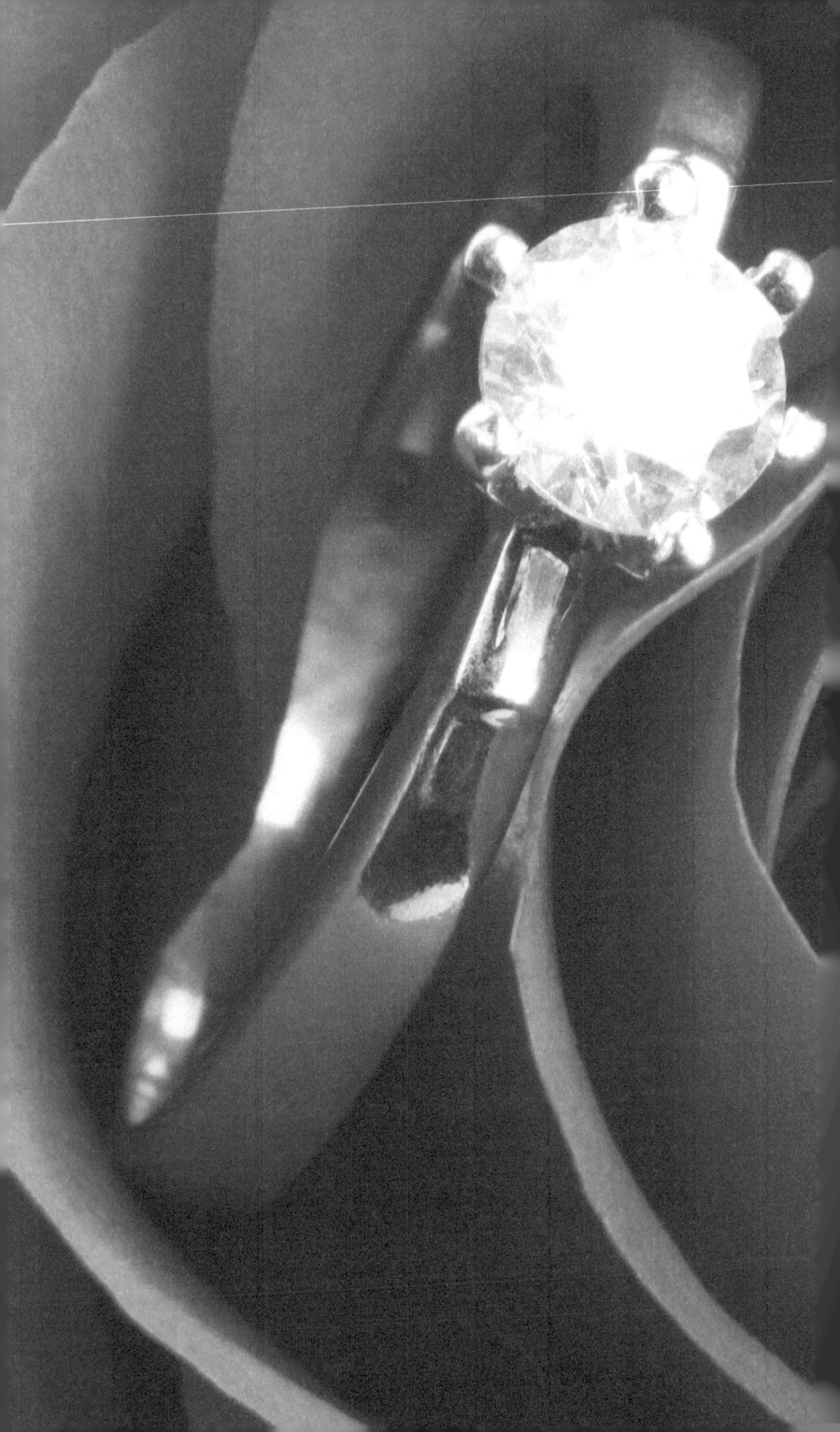

CHAPTER FIVE

CLAUDIA

THE MEDICS WORK ON MY ARM, BUT ALL MY attention is focused on the man who saved my life. He's brooding in the corner, and then the truth falls from the cop's mouth. His face becomes darker, anger vibrating from his body. It's evil, but nothing I haven't seen before.

I'm afraid of him—as I should be. Still, when he approaches, I don't move. I accept his rage as he grips my throat in hateful spite. He believes I've set him up, and when I look at it from his perspective, I can see it, but I'm not capable of such duplicity.

I take his threat seriously, but there is something behind his eyes that makes me think he doesn't want to believe I've betrayed him. Maybe it's the last bit that gives him a hint of faith in me. Connor MacNamara desired me, even for a brief moment. I felt the same way, and damn myself, because I still do. It irritates me because it seems I have no backbone. He threatened to kill me if I betrayed him, and all I could think about was if he leaned in a little farther, our lips would touch. I'd have those angry, vitriol-filled lips on me and my body would burn like nothing I'd ever imagined.

"Claudia, Claudia," Nick calls out, rushing toward the ambulance. Ah, biscuits. Man, do I regret seeing him.

"What are you doing here, Nick?" Of all the people to be here when he works downtown.

"What do you mean? I got the notice from my people about your bakery."

"Your people?"

"I'm the head of law enforcement, Claudia, as the AG." I do my best to control my expression. He's here for my safety and I should be happy about that.

"I suppose that's true."

"How much blood have you lost, sweet thing?" I'm going to punch him in the head. Wow, I can't stand him. He makes my stomach turn with that endearment.

"Could you not call me that?"

"You are just flustered." He takes my hand, and then it hits him. "Where is your ring?"

"It's upstairs. I can't wear it while I'm working. It's safer to put away so it doesn't end up in the batter," I inform him.

"I don't like that. Maybe this is a sign that you shouldn't have this place. It's obviously not safe here. The gangs are out of control in this area. The cops are already under the impression that it was a drive-by." I don't give him any information on it because I know it will get back to my father. Either the police straight up lied to him or he's lying to me about what they told him.

"I don't want to have this discussion right now, Nick. I'm tired and in pain. I'd like to go to bed," I sigh, feeling the exhaustion and blood loss.

"I just told you it's not safe and you can't stay here," he hisses. There is no empathy or care in his tone. I want to cry, but I won't give him the satisfaction of showing any emotion.

"Well, I sure as hell can't stay with you. We're not married."

"When are you going to get over that virginal attitude? It's 2014."

"Yeah, well, we're not all promiscuous," I say, reminding him of what I walked in on. I can assure him that's not something I could ever forget. It was all front and center and a reminder of what kind of husband he'd make.

"She came onto me." Oh goodness, the excuse is terrible and makes me sick.

"Whatever, Nick. That was before we even started dating and frankly none of my business, but I still have my beliefs and if you can't respect that, then I'll have to call this off." I refuse to play this game with him.

"What? You can't." He takes my hands in his. "Please just go get your things, and I'll take you to your father's where it's secure—and don't forget your damn ring."

"Don't talk to me like that. You need to learn to respect me. I could have died today, and you're being hostile toward me. Wait for me." I enter my apartment, then get the ring from the drawer and pack a bag. When I come back down, Nick is gone. I walk up to one of the cops and ask, "Have you seen the AG?"

"Sorry, Miss Murphy, he asked that we take you to the governor's home. He had an important meeting he couldn't miss," he says, looking at me with pure pity. I deserved better. Nick and I were over, and I was ending it as soon as I felt better.

"Don't," I mutter. As much as I understood his sympathy, I didn't need him to feel bad for me. It was my choice to be a fucking doormat. "Please just take me there."

He takes my bag and drives me to my father's mansion. When I arrive, the guards are happy to see me and lead me in without a problem. They are fussing over me like they always do. He's currently in town for a meeting and then he'll be down in Springfield in two weeks, but then there's a special party next week, so he wants to parade Nick and me around.

I head up to my bedroom, which is the way I left it the last time I was here, so I lie down and rest. Sleep comes to me easily until I hear the bullets come through the glass, and I let out a high-pitched scream. I sat up in bed, finding that I was just having a nightmare. My heart beats rapidly like it's going to pop out of my chest.

There's a knock at my door, and I expect it to be my father to scold me for disturbing the family, but it's actually one of the guards. "Miss Claudia, are you okay?"

"Yes, just a nightmare."

He gives me a sympathetic smile. "Hopefully it will pass in time. Please get some sleep."

"I will. Thank you." I close the door and walk to my bathroom. My arm is killing me and the bandage is leaking a little, so I quickly clean it up and then take a pain pill before sliding back into my bed. This time sleep doesn't come as easily, so I lie in bed and contemplate all the things I need to do.

My bakery was riddled with bullets and is inoperable at the moment, not that Nick had given me a choice. My bakery was already being boarded up when I was leaving, so I couldn't even check it out. Still, I plan to examine it tomorrow and hope that my kitchen doesn't look like Swiss cheese.

I check my phone for messages and there are twenty, including some from clients who have pickups today.

I start making calls, apologizing for disappointing them and issuing refunds. I go along with the drive-by story because that's the best situation, and everyone is flabbergasted. After appeasing most of them, I finally lie back down and let sleep take over.

"Well, you finally made it out of bed. You shouldn't be so lazy, Claudia. It doesn't look well on the wife of the Attorney General," my father says when I enter the dining room as he eats his breakfast. He doesn't even have the decency to look up at me while he shits on me first thing in the morning.

"Are you serious? I was shot yesterday, and that doesn't look good as the wife of the AG," I toss back out, venom laced in my words.

"Oh, so you've come around to the idea," he answers as if the engagement part was the only thing he heard. I roll my eyes and immediately regret not schooling my expression.

His expression darkens, and I'm about to feel his wrath. "Young lady, you need to learn your manners."

"I'm sorry," I say, grabbing a glass for orange juice.

"We've announced the engagement this morning in the papers as a part of the shooting. Sadly, that means the press will have a field day with this." My mouth falls open, and I nearly drop my juice. "You need to get dressed in the best clothes you have here, and don't forget that we're going to the gala next week."

"Okay," I answer half-heartedly as I try to process it. My head is swimming, but I'm starving and not in the mood to argue.

"Okay?"

"Yes. I haven't forgotten any of this. I'm really tired, and I don't want to argue. I need to eat something before I take some more ibuprofen so my stomach doesn't get injured."

He raises his head from his paperwork and glares before he says, "No hard drugs. Can't have a druggie in the family."

"Enough. There is no hard stuff. Just antibiotics and generic over-the-counter pain meds because I had a bullet go through my body." I want to tell him to try it sometime and see if he'd take something for it. The jerk is ticking me off, but I can't shake my years of good behavior toward him.

He reaches out and pats my hand. "Of course. I'm sorry, sweet girl. Get some food and then rest." Sometimes I wonder if the man suffers from some mental disorder because he always blows hot and cold with me.

I STAND BETWEEN MY FATHER AND NICK, AND IN a smooth, bold move, Nick takes my hand in his as my father begins to speak. "Ladies and gentlemen, yesterday was a harrowing day for my daughter. However, thanks to the wonderful members of the Chicago Police Department and medical services, she's doing wonderfully and is here today to celebrate a special announcement. Attorney General Nick Mirren has asked my daughter to be his wife, and she has said yes."

The crowd of reporters immediately grows loud with questions through the light cheers of the few people there, but I see a pair of eyes in the crowd through the bright lights—or at least I swear I do, but then he's gone. Of all the people to be at the press conference, why would he show up? God, what must he be thinking? I want to rip my hand from Nick's, but I can't without causing a scene.

I want to shrink into myself as the reporters and all the news media ask way too many questions for my liking. Nick brings my hand to his lips, kissing the expensive ring. I'm not shocked by the public display because he wants everyone to see the piece without looking like a pervert. They ask about the massive age gap between us, and he says, "Sometimes love just overshadows everything else."

"Miss Saunders, do you have anything to say?" A woman I recognize for her staunch opinion on men. She's a ballbuster and I'm sure she'd love the scoop, but it's not in my best interest to say a damn thing.

"Sorry. I'm still not feeling well after yesterday, but thank you for your well wishes."

"My daughter has been through a lot, but we just wanted to reassure you she is fine and will be well. Thank you for your support. Now, we need to get her some rest." My father uses that statement as an effective way to end the press conference outside of city hall.

They lead me out with gingerly love, like they care and of course it's all for the cameras.

As we get into the armored limo, my father glares at me, yanking my wounded arm. "You could have put on a more enthusiastic performance."

"You know I don't like the media, and I really don't feel good." They both look at me and notice my color has paled. My arm is bleeding again. "I think my wound is open again." And then I black out, behind my eyelids I picture Connor protecting me with his larger frame.

CHAPTER SIX

CONNOR

My teeth grind together as I watch that fucker take her hand. If I could put a bullet between his eyes, I would. Can't he see that she is distressed? That she is on the verge of fainting and doesn't want to be anywhere near there? Is she recoiling from his touch, or is that my foolish pride thinking I had some sort of effect on her? She wasn't wearing a ring yesterday when we met, but she is today. His fucking ring.

I miscalculated the calculating little wench. My gut burns thinking about how badly I was going to forget all my hatred for Saunders to fuck her.

"Are you following them?" I contacted Mac who has been following her since the shooting. I put a tail on her to see if she was involved and if she was working with her piece-of-shit father. So far, she's been up her father's ass, and that asshole Mirren has been at his home all day.

"Yes. They aren't going back to his mansion or the AG's place. It looks like they're headed to Northwestern," Mac says.

"The university?" I ask. Does she take classes, or does he have another presentation?

"No, the hospital."

"What the fuck?" Shit, is she that ill? She didn't look good on the stage, but that isn't my problem. My phone is buzzing with a call on the other line.

"Keep your eyes on her. I have business to attend to. We need to find out who set me up." I end the call and take the new one. "What's going on, Jack?"

"Are you going to come over for dinner tonight?" he asks as if there's no other care in the world. I know he's fucking all happy, but I'm in the middle of a big mess if he's forgotten.

"Yes. I have a lot to talk about just in case you've forgotten."

"Good. John misses you, and no I haven't asshat."

"I doubt it." As much as I love my little brother, I'm not sure he remembers me like he does Jack. It seems I'm not a part of his life, even when I'm right there. I try, but it's as if he doesn't see me.

It hurts, but I get it now more than before. Nora explained that sometimes kids like him pick one person to focus on and that's it, but if I slowly keep trying with gentle movements, he'll let me in. He used to let me participate, and he wasn't screaming with me like he was with my father, but he shines with Jack. Then again, Jack was always a surrogate father to all of us.

He sighs. "Don't do that. John loves you in his own way."

"I know that now." It's still not easy, but Jack and Nora have it a lot harder. Raising John takes a lot of love and patience and they're great at it.

"So how is it going with the bakery issue and his daughter?" About time he asked me.

"She's fucking engaged to the attorney general."

"What? Mirren?" he gasped out loud.

"Yes. That creepy fuck."

"I thought..." he stops himself, but I'm not letting that go.

"What? What did you think?" I questioned.

"Nothing. I just thought you two looked close in the ambulance. I could have sworn she wanted to chase after you when you stormed away."

"All women want to chase after me, but that doesn't mean she's not engaged. Hell, she wasn't wearing a ring. Maybe she takes after her father," I scoffed.

"Maybe, she was playing a really good game yesterday."

"Yeah." I get a pain in my chest that I can't explain. I'm only thirty-four and in great health, but I'm wondering if I need to see a doctor. "I've got to go."

"Business at the docks?" he asks.

"Yes."

"Okay. Six."

"Yes, I'll be there." My drive to the docks to handle the supply of goods is quick despite the midday traffic. As I pull up to my freight container, the weather shifts from a sunny sixty-five to a dark, wet fifty-seven. "Shit," I grumble. My men are already there, waiting for me.

"Eddie, Jimmy, were there any problems?"

"None, except for this fucking rain." They open the container, and inside is the new seating for the club. All the best fine Italian leather—shit that I don't want ruined from the rain.

"We're sorry about the weather, Mr. MacNamara. We've inspected the imports, and now that you have too, we can have it moved onto the trailer to be shipped to the location listed on the load sheet. We just need you to sign off." Jimmy stands outside while Eddie and I take a better look at two pieces that are deeper in the container, finding just what I'm looking for, fully stocked.

We exit, and I sign off on the docks as my men lock the container back up, taking the keys with them. "Please alert me when this arrives. Do not unload until the rain ceases. The club is closed until the weekend, so I'll be there to inspect it tonight, if the weather is clear, or first thing in the morning."

"Yes, boss." I shake the dock manager's hand and leave.

My men know damn well what is going on. After dinner tonight, we'll have the new weapons we acquired from Russia. Running back to my vehicle, I slosh through the rain, which only grows heavier, and I make it back to my SUV soaking wet. This is bullshit. I take off my drenched coat and set it on the heated seat to dry off while I hit the road. Now to return home.

A call from my man on her comes in just as I'm five minutes from the family estate. "What's up, Mac?"

"Sir, she's out now. I looked in and spoke to a cute nurse who I was able to pump some information out of. She told me that her bullet wound was re-aggravated, and she needed it stitched up."

"How did it happen? I saw her on stage."

"Yeah, it seems the nurse noticed handprints on her arm that were quickly covered." My temper heats up. I know one of those fuckers must have done it.

"What the fuck?" I snarled, feeling the leather of the steering wheel crack under the pressure of my fingers.

"Yes. Someone applied pressure."

"Watch her closer. If they even raise their voice to her, kidnap her ass."

"Understood."

CHAPTER SEVEN

CLAUDIA

It's time for the gala and I don't want to go, but I know there will be hell to pay if I don't. Right now, I'm hanging on by a thread both emotionally and physically. All I have is my father and Nick, even if they aren't the men I want in my corner. The only other man I know and strangely crave wants me dead.

Thankfully I was able to go back to my apartment and my bakery to at least salvage some of my upcoming orders. Most of my kitchen is fine. There were only two bullets that had gone into the kitchen area, and they hadn't done any serious damage to the equipment. It's the storefront that has been completely destroyed, and of course my arm, which had almost been lost. The trip to the ER was a big deal. Now, I'm here, putting on a show like nothing's wrong when I only want to be in bed.

I think about how it could have been my life. My heart races at how I wake up in pure fear every night. The only thing I can think of are the blue eyes with pupils that were fully dilated with adrenaline as he stared at me, pinning me to the ground while demanding I stay there. I try not to think about him, but every night Connor invades my dreams like a twisted hero.

The man hasn't left my mind since we met, and I can't believe how much Connor has affected me. The way he protected me had shown me more respect than my own family and even my supposed fiancé.

Dressing for the event, I pick a gorgeous blue number that matches the eyes of my savior who has left a twisted ache inside me. Why I expect him to be there, I can't understand. The event is exclusive to the city's developers and financial backers on major construction projects. It's being held at a lakefront property that just opened after multiple investors put in to make it happen. It's a crown jewel for the city and will host offices and several fancy restaurants.

"This place is gorgeous," I whisper before we exit the limo.

My father leads the way with a local district attorney as his date for the evening. Nick takes my hand, and we enter the event. Cameras are all over us, getting as many shots as possible. "You look radiant, Claudia. Are we going to be expecting a baby soon?" The question takes me by surprise.

"Is that what the trip to the hospital was for?" Another reporter shouts.

"There are pregnancy rumors?" I asked Nick.

He turns to the press with his usual charming smile and says, "Enough. My sweet girl isn't pregnant, but we will be starting a family as soon as we're married, right, sweet girl?"

"When I'm married, I'll consider children," I answer diplomatically. This marriage isn't happening as far as I'm concerned. As soon as I have the strength, I'm running away from them. Before the shooting and admittedly before Connor, I had no damn backbone, but something in me changed and I can't explain it.

"AG Mirren, may I have a word with you both?" a man I don't know asks, gesturing to my father.

"Dear, please excuse us." Nick kisses my cheek and then steps away, dragging his hand along my back as he does. Damn, do I need a drink. I walk over to the waiter who is holding a tray of champagne and then snatch a glass.

"Why, don't you look like the perfect fiancée, Miss Murphy," a voice I can't forget whispers against my ear as my lips touch the glass. I turn around to see Connor MacNamara standing in the room wearing a tie that matches my dress as if we coordinated. He's standing by a beautiful woman who makes me want to scream. She's perfect with her chocolate hair curled hanging over one shoulder.

Another handsome man comes up on her other side and slides his hand around her waist. "Thank you for watching my fiancée, brother," he remarks. So, she's Nora. Oh my goodness, she's even more beautiful than I imagined.

"And who is this?" he says with a devilish smirk as if he already knows the answer to the question. I have a feeling he's the type of man that always has the answers.

"Let me introduce you to the little devil herself—Miss Claudia Murphy, or rather, should I say Miss Saunders, or is it soon-to-be Mrs. Mirren?" I flinch at the last bit.

"A devil? It would take one to know one, Mr. MacNamara. And here I was hoping to thank you for saving my life. Although, I must say it was probably your fault I was shot in the first place, but since you're a jerk, have a good night." I move to turn on my heel and he reaches out, sliding his hand around my waist, pulling my body firmly to his.

His voice is low as he leans in and says, "I don't know which act is real—the little tough girl, or the little sweet girl."

I shiver in revulsion at that nickname. "Don't ever call me that again. Release me, now." I step on his foot with my heel, and he unhooks his hand from my waist.

I storm away, hating how much I want to cry. For him, I'd gladly be sweet, but my father and Nick ruined it. I need to find the bathroom or maybe get some air. Remembering that there were too many photographers outside, I chose the bathroom, but the path there was crowded, so I looked for another one.

"Excuse me. Is there another restroom?" I asked one of the servers.

"Yes, down that hall." She points, and I thank her before making my way down the hall.

The light sound of raised voices behind a door draws me closer. Then, the man who called my father and Nick away exits a room. I duck to the side and hide in a small alcove where it's dark and a large potted plant makes for a great hiding spot, and he doesn't see me. My father and Nick don't follow. I wait another moment and then move closer to the door where the guy left it ajar. I see my father and Nick in a private conversation.

Nick tosses back a drink so fast. "I can't believe that piece of shit showed up here," my father says, fists clenching before he straightens them and runs one through his hair. Damn, he must be pissed if he's going to mess up his hair.

"Did you see the way he looked at me?" Nick gasps. That was fear in Nick's voice. Who are they talking about?

"Yes, I didn't miss it."

"He probably thinks I'm the one who put the hit on him since he has eyes on my woman. He has no idea it was you." They are talking about Connor and me. Did he just say my father's the reason I was shot? I nearly reveal my position with a gasp, but I catch myself.

My father chuckles hard. I miss something he said, but then he continues, "He has a lot of fucking nerve. You think that shooting up my daughter's building would have done the trick to keep him away from her, but he's here anyway with his eyes on her too."

"We'll make sure that can't happen after tonight," Nick says. What the hell does that mean?

A shift happens in me, and I've had enough of this timid behavior. I open the door and stare down my father and my jackass fiancé. "What? I can't believe you did that." They both spin toward me with wide eyes.

"It's not what you think," my father exclaims, trying to look past me.

"So, you're telling me that you had nothing to do with the shooting?" I challenge, glaring at him while standing against the door so they can't escape.

"Well," he drags out the word.

"Answer me," I bark out, anger dripping from my words. "Answer me now, damn it."

"It's complicated."

"It's not complicated, *Dad*." As the air fills with tension, I consider another idea. "How did you know that they were gonna be there? I never told anyone about it, and I especially wouldn't talk about my work with you." I don't have any business partners, so nothing is shared.

"Well, I got a look at your schedule," he confesses. The son of a bitch. If I was ballsier, I'd slap him or kick him in the nuts.

I shake my head. "You mean you hacked my computer. I can't believe you would do something that crazy. I could have been killed." The tears I'd been holding back earlier are back again. There are a lot of things I believed he was capable of, but this was a whole new level of betrayal.

"But you weren't."

"Yes, thanks to the man you tried to kill." I jab my finger in his chest, trying to fight back tears. Connor was right. He'd been set up and I was a part of it, even if it wasn't the way he thought. I'm a pawn in a bigger scheme to get to their family.

"And you. What was the point of asking me to marry you if he was planning to kill me?"

"We weren't planning to kill you," Nick says. "The guy was an excellent marksman. The asshole got you shot by getting in the way and since he failed, he paid the price. Connor MacNamara wasn't supposed to see the shot coming and should be dead. Instead of being shot, you could have gone about your day with a messy outfit." Is he really being this cavalier about it?

I shake my head, flabbergasted, incensed, and completely heartbroken. "I can't believe this."

"Please believe that I don't want you dead, my sweet girl, and neither does Nick. I need my legacy to continue on. Your babies will be my grandchildren and the hope of my future, so the sooner you two tie the knot, the better."

"Excuse me, but this room isn't for use," someone says, knocking on the door. Nick walks to the door.

"Forgive us, we needed a private family moment," he explains to the person at the door.

"I'm sorry, Mr. Mirren, Governor Saunders."

"We're coming right now. Are you feeling better, sweet girl?" He reaches for me, but I move out of his grasp.

I wipe my tears away. "Yes." I step out ahead of them and say, "Please show me to the ladies' room."

"We'll meet you in the ballroom."

"Of course. I only need a moment to freshen up." She shows me the way to the ladies' room, which is crowded with many other women who have gathered. I take myself to a stall for some privacy. Breathing deeply, I brush strands of loose hair out of my face. What should I do? I can't leave with my father or Nick, but I can't give them a reason to think I'm going to run either. I open the bathroom stall door and exit to the sink in front of me. That's when I spotted Nora.

"Oh, excuse me."

"Are you okay?" she asks.

"Yes, I'm fine." This isn't how I thought my first real meeting with Nora would go. I'm a pathetic mess and she's the prime example of elegance and control.

She presses her hand on forearm and gives it a gentle squeeze. "Are you sure? I'm sorry about Connor's behavior. After everything that's happened this past year, the men don't have a lot of grace to give people, and I'm afraid that you made it a bit messy for him."

"I'm sorry. Things are crazy for me right now."

"Let me know if you need anything."

"I...thanks." I was going to say that I can't use my phone, but I'm not sure if my father has access to it. She steps out of the bathroom, and I mentally prepare myself as I wash my hands.

It's been a week, and my arm still burns, but it's nothing compared to the sting in my chest or the rage in my soul. I've always been the good girl, Daddy's little princess. The governor's daughter who hid under the radar. Kept my mouth shut and my legs closed, but those days are over. Unfortunately, I don't have a leg to stand on unless I find an ally. My enemy's enemy is my friend, or if I get my way, my fiancé —

CHAPTER EIGHT

CONNOR

LETTING HER WALK AWAY HAD TAKEN MORE willpower than I possessed. If she hadn't stepped on my foot, I wouldn't have let her escape my grasp. Then I spotted her asshole father and fiancé leaving the same area I saw her go into moments earlier. Where had she disappeared to?

"She's in the ladies' room, jerk," Nora remarks.

"What? She's the one who stepped on my foot."

"Yes, when you physically accosted her after you insulted and accused her of things," she huffs. "By the way, she was crying in there, or at least fighting off tears."

"What?" What's worse is I'm not sure who caused them. It could be because I'm a prick, but what did those assholes do to her?

"Yeah, but whatever you do, don't make a scene because their guards are all around and you know damn well they'd like nothing better than to find a reason to arrest you," Nora says.

"Well, they mustn't know that this is my property, my dear. If you need to get your troublesome thing alone, I can make it happen," my brother adds, squeezing her hip.

"I'd like that very much. In fact, I'll be waiting in our private offices upstairs," I say, making my way to the elevator and over to my office, which is set up next to my brother's.

It's not long before a message comes from Jack. *Your little cupcake is on her way up.*

There's a light knock on my door a moment later. "Come in."

The door opens slightly and then she comes in nervously, looking around. When she sees me behind the desk, she closes the door behind her. "Lock it," I insist.

God, does she look so damn good in that dress. I want to tear it off her and lick her from head to toe. "To what do I owe the pleasure of your presence, Miss Murphy?"

She cocks her brow, walking toward the desk, but stopping a few feet in front like she doesn't trust me enough to get closer. That's fine because I'll have her where I want soon. "I was asked to come see you, but as it happens, I wanted to discuss a matter with you."

"And that would be?"

"We have an enemy in common," she states calmly.

"Only one?" I question, tipping my gaze to her hand, wanting to know which one of the assholes she hated because she is still wearing that fucking rock on her finger. I want to rip it from her finger and tell her she doesn't belong to another man, but that's not the case.

"Well, then, I believe two is more like it. However, one has crossed the line and is unforgivable." She pauses, taking a deep breath, and says, "He orchestrated the hit on you."

"Oh?" I stand and round the desk. Standing in front of her, I take her hands and sit her on the edge of my desk. "Tell me what happened."

"My dad…he hacked my computer. He knew your brother and Nora would be there and didn't care if I got caught in the crossfire. Although, he said that the guy was a marksman, so I wouldn't have gotten shot if you didn't force me to duck."

"Fuck." I stand back and then rub my hand over my face. I don't know if I should tell her the truth. The fucker was caught on camera, and he's no damn marksman. He is a lowlife thug who has a criminal record and bad aim. He's up for two murders and out on bail. This is his ticket out of town. He failed, and they found his body in an alley in the territory of the rival gang he killed.

"I know you still blame me, but I swear I didn't—"

I cup her cheek, effectively silencing her. "I don't blame you, Claudia. Thank you for telling me."

There's a pounding on my door. "MacNamara, where is my daughter?" my father roars.

Her eyes widened. "Excuse me, Governor, but what are you doing up in the private offices? You don't have any reason to be up here. This is a business space and not a part of the party area," I hear my brother say.

"Another piece of scum. What are you doing here?"

"Scum, sir? This is my property. My brother and I invested in this property to help the city that we love. Now, if you'll please rejoin the party, I'm sure your daughter is down there with her fiancé unless he was off chasing that redhead I saw him with before I came up here."

"That's just his former assistant." Claudia's eyes turn to slits, and she covers her mouth. She's about to go to the door, but I slip my hand around her waist.

I lean in and whisper in her ear, "Don't you move an inch. Our conversation isn't over, and if you walk out that door, you know he'll keep close tabs on you." My breath is so close to her skin it blows light strands of amber golden hair away from her neck and sends tiny shivers down her body.

"They left," she says when the elevators are gone.

"Yes, but where does it leave us?"

"As of right now, I don't know. Now, I must return and not make a scene, but I'll be in touch soon."

"How's your arm?" I rub her shoulder above her injury, wanting to kiss her pain away.

"It's better," she whispers as our eyes meet. Her tongue peeks out from her lips and I have to swallow hard because if I kiss her, she's not leaving until her pussy is flooded with my nut.

"Come on, we need to get you back downstairs."

We exit together, and I drop her off a floor above the party to take the stairs with my guard watching so she can return to the ladies' room unbothered. Her father and fiancé are monitored and are busy talking to someone else when I reappear and speak to Fieri, who introduces me to Mirren as if I don't know the asshole. The damn asshole governor just blurts out, "Where is my daughter?"

"Excuse me, sir, but keep your voice down. Second of all, I haven't spoken to your daughter since I arrived and she told me to fuck off. I was in my office on an important business call when I heard you shouting down my building. Some manners go a long way. If you keep this up, I'll have you escorted out in front of everyone, including that cute but spoiled little shit of a daughter of yours. The apple doesn't fall far from the tree, I suppose."

"Watch your mouth when you speak about my fiancée." She comes up just as Nick says that, giving me a shitty look. I toss up the palms of my hands.

"Sorry, my bad. Have a good evening, gentleman, Miss Murphy," I add with a scoff. "I need a drink and a hot woman," I say, walking away, hoping they didn't think she was with me.

"Where were you?" I hear her father snap.

"I was stopped by one of the women wanting baking tips, so we walked over into a quiet alcove where she took notes and while a waiter fed me some champagne." She giggled with a glass of wine that was almost gone. "I'm on my third glass, but it made me have to pee again, and this dress isn't the easiest to use the bathroom in." She winks at them. I do my best to observe from my stance in the group behind them. I smile at her antics. Damn, she's better at fooling them than I gave her credit for.

"You're on pain meds. You shouldn't be drinking like that," he reminded her.

"Well, you hurt my feelings, Daddy," she huffs out, sounding wasted.

"I'm sorry, my sweet girl." I make note of that.

"I hate when you call me that." She downs the glass, then snatches another off the waiter's tray.

"See? You're not in your right mind," the governor insists, keeping his voice low so as to not cause a scene.

"I need to go home."

My brother stalks closer to her with a scowl on his face. "Yes, you do. Miss Murphy, my brother just informed me that you're a minor and that you weren't allowed to consume that."

"I'm twenty-one. My birthday was two days ago. I was shot on my birthday. I didn't tell you that, did I, Mr. MacNamara."

"Call for a car for Miss Murphy," Jack insists, and I smirk because he's playing it perfectly for me. It works for my plans while mitigating the drama at the moment. I have plans for the little baker, and I will have them pay, but I don't want them to see how eager I am for Claudia.

"She doesn't need a car. I can take her home," her father offers, but I doubt he means it.

"Actually, sir, you're due for a speech in twenty minutes." I watch the AG's eyes move, and they go straight to the redhead in the corner before flitting back to his fiancée.

"Oh, come on. I'll take your offer, Mr. MacNamara. My fiancé tells me to forget how I met him with his dick buried in his assistant, but it's obvious he hasn't forgotten." She yanks the ring off her finger. "Here you go. Give this to her since it's what you both want, and I'd rather be shot again than be your wife. I'm done. Bye."

Her father grips her wrist and twists it, stopping her in her tracks. She lets out a little yelp, but the party is so loud no one has been privy to our mini scene. I lean in and pinch the nerve on his hand. "I could gladly rip your throat out. Let her go right now."

"She's my daughter and until tonight, she's been an angel," he tells me as if I'm the motherfucking problem as he releases the hold on her.

"That's before I found out my dad was willing to sacrifice my life for his own agenda," she hisses, lifting her chin up.

"You're insane. I think it's all these meds you're taking, Claudia. I don't know where you got that idea from."

"I'm tired," she sighs.

"Time to go," I insist.

"I'll take care of this. You take her home. Your driver is already waiting for you," Jack says.

"I will." I take her hand and lead her to the exit as we start to draw attention to ourselves. The second we're outside, the press begins to take photos. It's then that she loses her footing. I catch her and sweep her into my arms. More cameras go off, which piss me off because she's clearly not in a good place and they're taking advantage of it. The valet has the door open, and we climb inside. I buckle her in and sit beside her.

"I could kill those bastards," I snarl the second the door is closed.

"Sorry about that, boss. It's not like I could just shoot them," Joe, my driver and security says.

"No, you're right, but it still pisses me off."

"Take us to the estate." His brows raise and I stare at him, wondering why he's not moving. He gets going and then I give my attention to the gorgeous bit of trouble in my arms.

"Connor, I'm sorry. That's the first time I've ever had a drink," she confesses, looking adorable and lost.

"Oh, you are a mess, aren't you?" I say, brushing my hand down her face.

"Sorry. Don't be mean to me," she sighs, pressing her head onto my chest. It feels so good, but I ignore the situation because she's wasted, and as much as I'd like to fuck her cute ass, I'm not going to touch her until she's ready to toss her sexy body at me completely sober. She's a complicated woman and the daughter of my enemy.

I want her father dead, and as much as she says she hates him while she's drunk, she doesn't really hate him. No— tomorrow, the pretty little princess will want his love and attention, willing to forgive him. I won't allow her to forgive him because he'll be dead, but then she won't forgive me.

The moment we pull up to my house, she's wide awake and feeling a bit frisky. Claudia's clearly still inebriated, but she thinks she's sober. "You're sexy even when you're mean, Connor."

"Thanks, gorgeous," I answered, opening the front door.

She looks around in wonder and then confusion. "This isn't my apartment."

"Yeah, if you think I'm letting you back there in your condition, you're out of your mind. You're not sober, and your father and ex-fiancé are probably fuming now."

"Oh my goodness. They're going to want my head for today." She gasps and clings to my side as we enter my mansion.

"Wow, this is insanely perfect." Cain comes barreling through the house and directly toward her. "Whoa." She clings to me as expected when a hundred-pound dog comes at you.

"Calm down. Sit, Cain." He sits and wags his tail like a greedy little bitch. Some protector, but then again, he knows that she belongs here. "He likes you."

"Aren't you a good boy," she coos, reaching slowly and cautiously to pet him. He allows it and the more she digs into his fur, the more he pushes his head into her hand.

"Looks like you have an admirer."

"He's a big, adorable brute." She smiles kindly toward him and then looks up at me, and I want to kiss her but tell myself she's borrowed trouble. My end goal doesn't include her.

"Come on, let's get you in bed."

"I'm not sleeping with you just because my fiancé is a cheating bastard."

"Ex-fiancé, and I meant to sleep, baby girl." I swat her behind and lead her up the stairs.

"Hey," she gasps, turning her head with parted lips that will haunt my dreams tonight.

"Well, get moving, Trouble."

"You're the one who is trouble. A menace. A big man-ass," she says with a giggle. I don't know how drunk she is, but she's adorable. The fact that she just called me a big ass. A man who willingly kills people. Didn't her father mention she was taking pills too?

"How many pills did you take today?"

"My dad gave me two because I would be out for a long time tonight, and I was wearing heels and he didn't want me to complain about the pain," she explains, letting out a yawn.

"Fuck. What kind of pills?"

"I'm not sure. I think the bottle was labeled Vicodin." My mind whirls because even though Claudia was shot and that shit is brutal, she doesn't have a broken bone and it was a through and through that she didn't even go to the hospital for. She has full use of her arm.

"Baby girl, do me a favor. Wash up, and I'm going to get you a change of clothes."

"I'm going to make a call." She's a bit staggered for a minute as she stands. "You know what? Don't move." I walk into the other room. "Hey, Doc. I need you to come here. I think someone's been drugged, but I don't know what she has in her system. I need to know, so if you could, please get some bloodwork."

"Some blood tests won't tell you everything if it's in the system. I'm going to need a urine sample as well," he says.

"How long will it take for you to get here?"

"Twenty minutes to get there."

"Shit, she'll be passed out by then," I tell him, rubbing my hand on my chin, feeling my scruff coming in.

"Then find a clean cup and make her piss in it," he says, shaking off the sleep in his voice.

"Come on, baby girl." I step back into the room at the wrong time. Claudia is standing at the foot of the bed with the tight-ass dress over her head and her pink panties showing me what I want. I bit down on my bottom lip, fighting the urge to tackle her onto the bed.

"I'm stuck," Claudia grumbles through the sparkly fabric.

"Shit." I quickly move in front of her and grab the dress and tear.

"Hey, that costs a lot of money," she complains.

"I'll buy you a new one," I answer, looking down at her, and realize my mistake instantly. Fuck. She's not wearing a bra, and her massive tits are on display now, lightly touching the edge of my suit.

"Okay. Let me get you some clothes."

I move toward my drawers, but then her next words stop me in my tracks. "Do you always run away from women?"

"You're wasted and are trouble. As much as I'd love to pop those fat tits in my mouth before dropping you down onto your knees, I'll pass."

"That's not nice." Fuck. She looks so hurt and pouts, and I reach out and tug on her bottom lip. She has no idea how tempted I am to give in to every lustful thought I have right now. She's in my bedroom, a stupid move on my part because I could fucking stuff my cock deep in her pretty little mouth right now and almost not feel guilty, but she's not in her right mind.

"I'm not a nice man, baby girl. I'm an ass."

"I don't need clothes. You're not going to fuck me anyway, and I'm hot and tired." She plops on the bed, nearly missing the edge.

For some reason, the thought of the young doctor coming in here and seeing those perky tits that I haven't sucked on, haven't marked as my property yet, pisses me off. I don't even want her like that, but I still want to fuck her. "You fucking need clothes. The doctor will be here soon."

"I don't need a doctor." I take off my suit jacket and walk over to my drawers to look for a shirt, pulling out a simple tee before tossing it at her.

She holds it in her hands and brings it to her nose, breathing it in with a smile on her face. "You always smell so good."

"Like I said—trouble," I grumble, adjusting my dick.

Claudia sits there for a moment too long before I lose patience and close the distance between us. I grab the hem of the shirt and say, "Put this on, and you need to stay awake for the doctor to come."

"But I'm...tired..." She yawns as she slowly puts the shirt on. The sleepy thing drives me nuts.

"Okay, we're going to the bathroom together." I help her up and we get the job done.

CHAPTER NINE

CLAUDIA

Last night was a bit of a blur, but I hazily dreamed of Connor kneeling between my legs with water running. My eyes shoot wide open. "It wasn't water running. I was peeing. He had a cup under me in the toilet while I peed," I screech.

"Yes, a whole new experience for me too," he says from the doorway. My eyes briefly flit to him as he smirks with his arms crossed. How can he look so good with his white dress shirt sleeves rolled up and arms crossed?

"Why?" I ask, staring at the puzzling mobster. He is gorgeous, evil, and kind. A mixture that I can't understand because the dark side had only come out when he thought I betrayed him. Before that and even after, he'd shown me moments of pure gentleness, a feeling that did dirty things to my innocent yet broken heart.

"You were wasted last night. Completely fucking wasted," he grumbles, pushing himself off the doorframe and adding to his height. My body reacts, and I'm grateful that I'm still under the covers because then he can't see how wet my panties are.

"So, you decided to play doctor? That's not how I envisioned that game would go."

He scoffs, "No, Trouble. The doc wanted a urine sample, but you wouldn't stay awake. I'll be in my office. It's downstairs and to the left." He leaves the room and closes the door.

I really know how to push my luck with him, but I'm not sure how to act around him. He makes me want to stand strong, and then the next second I want to fall at his feet and do as he commands.

I look around and see that it's definitely a masculine room, and then I remember a bit more of last night. We laid in bed together. He wrapped his arms around me. The feel of his muscles coiling around my abdomen warms me back up, and I nearly doze back to sleep as the memories flood me.

"Watch over her," someone else said.

"I will." I remember him coming back and lying back down in bed. *I curled up in his arms, and he held me tight to his chest.*

I looked up at him and said, "What would you say if I wanted my father dead?"

He tilted his head down and said, "I'd say ask me again in the morning. Then we can strike a deal. Now go to sleep."

"Okay," I muttered sleepily. He chuckled, and I noted that I could fall in love with that sound.

Did I still want that? I have to think about it. Sitting up in bed, I looked for my phone and found my purse, which Connor was sweet enough to leave on the nightstand. I didn't even know I had brought it back with me.

I pull out my phone, and there are ten missed calls from my father and Nick, combined with a few texts.

Where are you?

Feeling bold, I respond to my father. ***None of your business, but let's just say Connor's not going to let you take me from him.***

I'm calling the FBI and reporting that he kidnapped you. I laugh at the threat because it's foolish since I can tell them he tried to kill me.

And I'll tell them that you are the one who had me shot and that you're the reason I had to go back to the hospital to get my wound restitched. Bye, Daddy. He doesn't respond again because he probably realized he's lost.

Do I want my father dead? Yes. I do. My father tried to have me killed more than once and is trying to force me to marry a cheating bastard, and all he cares about is his reputation.

I walk downstairs to his office in just his shirt and my panties, feeling exposed. Thankfully, there was no one around to see me half-naked. "Please come in."

"Now, to what do I owe this pleasure?" he asks, clasping his hands together, steepling his fingers like the menacing criminal he is. The sensual mobster stares at me and I almost lose my nerve, but I can't just walk out the front door like this. A part of me wonders if he did it on purpose.

"I don't have any clothes except for this." I looked down at the shirt of his I'm wearing that barely covers my panties. I watched the way his eyes appreciated my figure, and I'm so glad that his shirt reached past my ass because my undies were soaked. Not that he didn't get a good visual yesterday, but I doubt that was attractive. "And you kind of ripped my dress last night."

He has the nerve to give me a smile filled with pride. "Oh, you remember that?"

"No, I tried to put it on this morning," I lied. The memory of me begging him for sex was pathetic and his threats to push me onto my knees came back to me like a burst of shame and lust. I still wanted him and ached for him to show me how to be pleased.

"Actually, it's this afternoon."

"Semantics. Anyway, I need to go home, but I have a problem. I'm kind of half-naked." He purses his lips and puffs his cheeks for a moment before blowing out the air.

"Well, I can ask my brother to have Nora bring over some clothes for you. I think you guys are close to the same size."

"I would say that too. She's a little bit shorter, but I think it would be okay. Thanks for everything." I rock back and forth on my bare heels.

"Is that all?" I bite my lip, thinking about the call with my father and his veiled threat, and the words just come out.

"Actually, do you remember what I said to you last night?" I asked.

"Which thing?" His lips twist up into a perverse grin.

"Not the sex. I was drunk." He shrugs it off like it's not a big deal and I suppose for a man as hot and powerful as him, pussy isn't hard to get.

"Well then, Miss Murphy, care to elaborate?"

"I want my father dead."

A smirk spreads over his face. "I do remember, but I don't believe you. Everything I know about you, everything I see, screams a sweet, good girl."

I narrow my eyes at him and stalk toward his desk, ready to bite him, but I just keep my hands down at my sides and grit out, "What did I tell you about calling me that?"

"Oh, that's right—you don't like that."

"They call me that."

Suddenly he becomes pensive. Then, he's on his feet, coming around the desk, his strong, tall frame standing directly in front of me, his hand sliding over my shoulder. "I have to ask you something, and I want an honest answer from you. Did your father touch you? I mean sexually."

"God, no," I gasp, shaking my head.

"I just wanted to know if that 'sweet girl' term bothered you because of that."

"I don't care if you don't believe me, but I want him dead, even if I have to do it myself."

"How do I know that this isn't some ploy to team up with him to get at me and my family?"

"Are you serious? After last night?"

"Last night was somebody who got fucked up at a party. Drunk people at parties act like fools. Public officials don't like scenes, and cheating bastards happen all the time. That doesn't mean you won't take his ass back, especially with how jealous you got last night." I watch the look on his face and see how irritated he is by the idea of Nick and me.

A plan comes to mind that would piss off my father and prove to Connor that I'm on his side. It was buzzing around in my head before I slammed way too many drinks too fast. "I have a plan. My father and Nick called my phone last night multiple times."

He grimaced. "I know. They were blowing it up last night like crazy. I almost answered them and let them know I was buried inside you, but I didn't want to ruin your plans to return to them."

"Actually, I don't know if you have a girlfriend or not, but I was thinking maybe you could pretend to be engaged, and that will completely piss off my father to the point where he would do something stupid and you could take him out. No one would suspect anything, because we are an item." His face twists comically in surprise, but then he smirks.

"What would I get out of this?"

"Well, you get to kill my father." He thinks about my offer, taking a long time, so I add, "It would be totally fake, of course."

He taps my chin. "Tsk, tsk. Oh, you're thinking too small, little girl."

"What do you mean?"

"An engagement can be broken; you saw how easy last night was. Besides, engagements mean you'll live alone until we get married, giving your father a chance to put his hands on you again." He knows about my father hurting me. Then, I remember about last night and my father's obviously rough grip on me in public. "Don't think I don't know what happened that day, after you left the press conference and ended up at the hospital."

"You know?"

"My security detail followed you." He's been watching me. My body lights up with excitement. "I told you I wanted to know who was involved in the attack."

"Oh." Well, there goes the joy I felt for like half a second.

"So, do we have a deal? A fake marriage, and in the end, I kill your father. Hell, maybe I'll throw in that ex-fiancé for good measure."

"Yes. I want him to pay for his attempts on my life, for trying to ruin my happiness, and for trying to make me miserable just because I don't want to be his puppet."

"Well, there's just one thing to do: sign the contract and make it binding." He crushes his mouth on mine. The kiss is rough, dominating, and nothing like I've ever experienced before. I fall into it, clinging onto his shirt, wanting more. I slide my hands up over his shoulders as he slips his tongue inside. He only pulls back to stare into my eyes. "There's no going back on this."

"I know," I say, nodding and moving back in for another kiss.

Connor sets me on the desk and pushes my thighs apart, sliding my panties to the side with his adept fingers. All his motions are quick and smooth. His mouth works quickly, crushing mine with his, so perfect, effortless, talented. Connor is everything a man should be and more. I am lost, craving his touch and afraid to admit the truth. This deal is worth more to me, and he's the man that I'm willing to give it to just to have my peace.

Connor will be my savior, and I'm grateful to him, so giving him this was worth it. He can sign it with my blood, and I will be grateful. He kisses me crudely, grinding his mouth on mine as he unleashes himself from his trousers. I feel his dick rubbing up against me. It was so long and smooth, my eyes catching a glimpse of it just as he kissed my neck. I knew it was large, but this is massive. He is going to tear me in two and somehow, I know I'll love it.

My biggest fear is becoming addicted because this is only temporary. Becoming Connor's wife, his lover, will only be a brief moment in time. What would happen afterwards? I can't think about that now because my senses are overwhelmed with his touch. He takes off the shirt I borrowed, leaving me almost naked. "Fuck, baby, you're so hot." He rubs it up and down my slit, getting it soaked with my need. It only arouses me more.

He pushes his way in, inch by inch, as if he needs to breathe every step of the way, and then he lunges, pressing his hands on the desk and growling fiercely. The burning pain is brief as he barrels through my untouched body.

One hand grips my hair violently as he stares into my eyes. "You're my sweet little virgin, aren't you? Fuck, you are full of secrets."

"Not anymore," I moan. "You tore through my last one."

"Good, I don't appreciate liars, Claudia." He presses his forehead to mine. His hands rub up and down on my thighs. The rough grip sends hunger pulsing through me.

He stills, holding me tightly "You feel so good, baby. Tell me. Tell me when I can move." Connor slowly kisses my neck and up to my lips. "Tell me, baby. I'm on the edge. I'm about to nut in your tiny little pussy. See, you better tell me when I can move again. Don't be shy, baby."

I flex around him, giving him what we both need. My body aches and in good places; my breasts tingle so I give them a squeeze, pinching them. A moan escapes my throat, and he growls with appreciation. "Fuck, Claudia, you have me close, baby. So damn sexy. Wrap those legs around me."

He clutches the back of my hair and pulls me tighter. His hands play on my lower back, pulling me closer as he grinds into me with his cock so deep inside me. I can barely breathe with each thrust stealing my breath. Intense and pleasurable all at once. This man owns my body right now and is dominating every second, and I want more—I crave it.

I screamed his name as I came. "Connor."

My body shakes around his, and my pussy clenches around his huge, thick, thrusting cock. My orgasm rips through my body, and I've never felt so alive. Our eyes meet, and I can see the lust-filled haze, and a deep, passionate smirk spreads across his face, knowing he's succeeded.

He swallows my lips in a deep kiss before pumping harder and faster and letting go, filling me up. A growling moan comes from him as he releases his own orgasm. We're breathing heavy, sweat on both our foreheads as he presses his to mine. So incredible.

CHAPTER TEN

CONNOR

"THAT'S THE FIRST WEDDING CONTRACT I'VE ever signed like that," she says, panting heavily with a light giggle. My hand wraps around her throat as anger floods me.

"You're never going to fucking sign a contract like that again." Her eyes brighten, and her pussy walls tighten around my cock that's still deep in her cunt. "Do you understand me?"

"Yes. I don't plan to have anyone killed, anyway." She rolls her eyes, and I slam my dick into her, annoyed by her intentional misinterpretation.

I squeeze my hand tighter around her slender neck and stare into her needy gaze. "God, you're trouble."

"Fuck, you're so big," she pants, hands gripping the edge of the desk for purchase.

"That's right, but you'll get used to me." By the time she does, she'll be so damn addicted to my cock, I'll have a hard time pulling her off my dick. I want her so damn insatiable to the point that all she wants when I get home is for me to sink into her warmth.

"We don't need to have sex," she insists, living in a foolish state of denial.

"We do, because you'll be my wife, and as long as you're my wife, I'm not going to be fucking anyone else. I sure as fuck expect your loyalty as well." I rock my hips, driving into her again, giving her another orgasm before shooting my hot seed into her womb. I know I'm being dangerous because her tight pussy isn't protected from my swimmers.

Reluctantly, I pull out and give her back the shirt, even though I love seeing her topless. I tuck myself away despite the fact that I want to be inside her all damn day, but she is probably sore.

We have a quick wedding to plan before the governor pulls some bullshit, like saying I kidnapped his daughter or some shit like that, which I wouldn't put it past him.

I have to call my brothers and get them down here for a ceremony, and hell, I even need that asshole father of mine here for the show. I'm sure that will get Saunders's goat to have my father at the wedding.

"Trouble, this wedding is going to be a quick one. I'll get you a pretty dress, but we're marrying with no damn fanfare." She nods. "You can jump in the shower, and Nora's going to bring something over in the next twenty minutes. Then, you girls can talk about a nice dinner or some shit for the wedding." I hate that she's already dressed. Well, partially dressed because those sexy legs are on display, and I can see the remnants of my handiwork sliding down between her thighs.

"Totally get it. We both know this isn't real, Connor," she sasses and tilts her head to the side with a roll of her eyes.

I'm not sure why I'm so damn offended by the way she dismisses the validity of the marriage, but I am. "Yeah. Well, then, we better be careful because that nut I left in you was pretty real."

"I'm on the shot." She winks at me.

"Sweetheart, being shot and being on the shot are two different things."

"I got on birth control months ago." I have questions, but she just strolls out of my office without answering the why. I bet it was for that bastard. She has plans not to get pregnant any time soon.

After losing my mother to childbirth, I'm not sure I want kids either. It's an irrational idea because my mother was older and shouldn't have had a baby at her age. Hell, I didn't even know she could get pregnant at fifty, but I guess for some women, it's possible.

"That's good to know," I mutter, letting her go upstairs without delay since we have a million and one things to do in a short time period.

I'm about to walk into my office when I see my housekeeper appear. "Mr. MacNamara, you have a guest in your home?" Her attempts to keep the horrified look off her face fail miserably. I bet she's shocked. Not once have I ever brought a woman home.

"Claudia is not just a guest. She's my fiancée." As expected, her mouth falls open. However, she quickly corrects herself which is good because an ounce of disrespect will not be tolerated.

"You're getting married, sir?" she asked, taken aback by the news which I'm sure will shock everyone.

"Yes. Now, if you'll excuse me, I have to take Cain out for a walk."

"Does your fiancée need anything, sir?" she questioned, correcting her initial reaction. That's a good start.

"Please prepare her a meal. I'm sure she must be hungry."

"Of course." She nods as she always does for me, and I know that things will work out.

I walk away and call my brother in the process. "When are you getting here? I need this wedding to take place now." Suddenly, I'm getting anxious. Is this what they call cold-feet? Or maybe it's the opposite? I'm more afraid of the wedding not happening.

I have been making plans since I woke up this morning. Although she might have thought it was her idea, I'd whispered it to her last night while she was falling asleep. It was best that she became my wife so they didn't have control over her, and I could give her what she wanted while keeping her protected.

"We're all getting ready. Even our piece-of-shit father is coming," he grumbles. Yes, a necessary addition to stick it to Claudia's father.

The doorbell rings five minutes later, and it's Nora with two big bags. "Where is the bride?" she asks.

"She's in our bedroom."

"Good." She grins from ear to ear. "You're not allowed to see her until the wedding. Help me get some things out of the back." We go to the SUV, and she has it loaded with a suitcase.

"You're not trying to sneak her out of here, are you?" I questioned, getting a bit nervous because Nora really likes Claudia.

"No, we have some wedding prep to do. Besides, I want her to have some choice. You gave us no damn time, Connor. This is a girl's wedding."

"Yes, but it's only temporary," I say, trying to make myself feel better about being a douche.

"He's right. It's only temporary," Claudia says. I whip my head around and snarl, seeing her still in the same outfit.

"What are you doing walking around like that?" I bark at her, both angry and horny at the same time.

"You didn't say anything about it earlier." I close the distance between us and grab her ass.

"That's because I wanted you to be agreeable. Now, go get your half-naked ass dressed before any of my staff or men see you like this. You're about to be my wife."

"Temporary," she reminds me again.

"Temporary or otherwise, I'll have to kill them." She gasps, then shakes her head but doesn't argue and goes up to get ready like she's told to.

"You sound like Jack." Nora taps me on the shoulder and rushes up the stairs like a bat out of hell, following Claudia. I chuckle and remember that the front door is open.

As I go to close it, Jack shouts, "What the hell? Hold up." He's holding John's hand.

"Whoa, I didn't know you two were coming so soon."

"I didn't want Nora to know, but we followed her out. Right, John?" Jack looks over at John, who doesn't say anything because he's staring at Cain who is now at my side.

"Dog. Dog. Dog." He rushes to Cain, but he's trained to react only when I tell him to, so he remains calm.

"We pet nice," Jack says. I drop down on my haunches and so does Jack, and we try to show John how to touch Cain. He giggles when Cain dips his head and brushes John's hand, bumping him a bit back.

"Excuse me. I need to check on some of the arrangements." I leave the foyer and head into my office. Pressing the button in my top drawer, the wall of cameras opens and I check the feed. I want to be able to monitor any trouble while I conduct the last bit of preparations for the wedding.

Before sleeping beauty woke up, I'd been on a mission to get the ball rolling. She isn't returning to her previous life no matter what she thinks. I have plans for her, and they don't involve Mirren and that bastard father of hers, unless both of those fuckers were six feet under.

My phone rings, and it's the gate. "The judge is here for the ceremony." I watch him pull up in his dark blue BMW and smirk. It's beautiful, and I'm sure after I'm done paying him for this swift wedding, he'll be able to buy another brand new one if he wants.

"Send him in." It's going to be a few minutes before he makes it to the house, but even so, I need to finalize everything. My men are moving around the house setting up the dozen seats needed, and I had a florist do a rush delivery. My plan has been in motion since before she even woke up this morning. My sweet Claudia had no idea that I had considered the plan when she was pinned to my desk in the office while she was still wearing that prick's ring yesterday.

The longer this carries on, the greater the likelihood that Mirren or Saunders could interfere. Those fuckers don't know when to quit. I won't let them on my property, and I was able to swipe Claudia's phone when she came downstairs to see me.

I read through her texts and see that she hasn't answered his messages in a good while, but the previous ones give me a feel of her tone.

Her last message came through from her asshole father ten minutes ago.

Where are you?

None of your business, but let's just say Connor's not going to let you take me from him.

I'm calling the FBI and reporting that he kidnapped you.

And I'll tell them that you are the one who had me shot and that you're the reason I had to go back to the hospital to get my wound restitched. Bye, Daddy.

I power it off and then tuck her phone in my suit jacket.

"Where the fuck is Ian?" I snap, forgetting that John's there as I stroll back into the foyer where they're hanging out with Cain. Jack smacks my bicep with the back of his hand.

"Sorry." Luckily, John's so engrossed with the dog that he doesn't notice my outburst.

"He's on his way. He has matters that require his attention and not your impromptu wedding that you rushed, considering you stole my damn wedding cake maker," he grumbles out that last part.

"Are you upset that I'm getting married first?" I tease my older brother.

"No, I want Nora to have the cake she desired."

"Maybe we can still work something out."

"Good. Besides, I thought you weren't ever going to get married until I saw you in the back of that ambulance. The way she had you by the balls, it was obvious. And damn, you want Nick's balls in your hand before you kill him." I hate Nick Mirren more than I should because he isn't anything but a place holder. Still, something about his stupid fucking face irritates me.

"Balls," John says. "Balls." He claps his hands together. Luckily, Nora won't know that he's talking about the wrong kind of balls. I try not to laugh, but I can't help it.

"Damn it. I didn't bring any with me, John."

"Nope, you left your balls at home, or are they in Nora's purse?" I smile at my brother, knowing that Nora owns him.

"Keep it up, and we'll see where yours are soon. You can pretend all you want and tell me that this is just a contract, a way to play your enemies, but we'll see."

"It is. I like being balls deep inside her, but that's a bonus," I remarked. I'm not in love with Claudia like Jack is with Nora.

"Wait, you fucked her?" Jack says in a hushed whisper.

"Yeah."

"You're playing a dangerous game. Someone's going to get hurt, and if it's not you, it will be her. You better be careful, Connor."

"I know what I'm doing." The doorbell rings, and I answer it. "Hello, Judge Samuels, please come in."

"Congratulations, Connor. Hello, Jack. Who is this young one?"

"He doesn't engage with others." John hides right behind my leg, which takes me by surprise. "He's our little brother, John."

"Oh, yes. The youngest MacNamara boy. Well, hopefully you all start producing a bunch of little ones to add to the brood. I've just added three grandsons to my family in the past four months. My daughters all married around the same time."

"Well, we're going for two out of the three. I'll be getting married in the next few weeks." The bell rings again, and hopefully this is the last time because I'm ready to get this show on the road.

When the door opens, it's both my brother and my dad, who I'm surprised to see together.

"You two came together?" Jack blurted out before I could.

"No, he was walking up when I arrived," Ian said. He pushes past our father and into the house. "So when are we getting this show started? I have shit to do, and I'd like to get on with it."

"Well, thanks for being so damn so supportive, bro."

"The day you marry because you love your wife and not because you want to get back at the fucking bastard that this asshole can't stop fighting with, then I'll give a shit. You deserve better than marrying trouble."

"You don't have to be here, Ian. Your brother is still going to marry her whether you like it or not," our father said.

"Boys, we're ready," Nora calls out from the top of the stairs.

"We're ready for my bride," I say, giving my brother a cold look. With a whisper, I warn, "Don't you dare disrespect her again."

"I'm sorry, Connor. I shouldn't have said anything about your bride regardless of my reservations," Ian apologized.

Nora leads the way down in a light blue dress, and then behind her is my bride in a pretty white dress that goes down to her feet. My heart pounds out of my chest. I can't believe the miracle Nora managed to work in a matter of three hours since I called this morning. She turned my gorgeous woman into a stunning bride that I know I don't deserve.

The room is silent as Claudia meets me at the bottom of the steps. "You look perfect, Trouble."

"Got to play the part when marrying my hero," she answers with a wink and a smile. I want to get our vows over with so I can carry her over my shoulder up to our bedroom and spear her with my big, fat cock.

Everyone sits and the Judge begins. "Ladies and gentlemen, we're gathered here to join Connor MacNamara and Claudia Saunders in holy matrimony by the power vested in me by the State of Illinois."

The judge continues with the quick ceremony, and in a matter of minutes it's time for me to kiss Claudia. I slide my hand into her honey brown hair and cup her head, tipping her lips up to mine. "Mine," I growl before I snatch our first kiss as husband and wife. It's a fast but possessive kiss that leaves no room for those in the room to doubt that she's my wife, whether it's my father or my brother, who clearly have objections.

"Congratulations, Mr. and Mrs. MacNamara. Please sign here," the judge says. I sign first and hand Claudia the pen for her to follow suit. She does, and I love the flawless effort in her pen stroke.

"Thank you," I say, addressing the judge. I shake his hand, and then I turn to my family. "Thank you all for coming to our wedding."

"It's a pleasure to meet you, Claudia," Ian says. "You make a lovely bride."

"Thank you, Mr. MacNamara."

"Call me Ian."

"Apparently I'm trouble, Ian. Don't worry, though. I'll play nice if you play nice." She winks at him with a load of sass.

"Damn, Connor. She's something else. I suppose I'll play nice."

"He's a good little puppy, isn't he?" my father mocks foolishly.

Ian's hand wraps around my father's throat before he can get another word out. "Old man, you're on your last fucking thread. What makes you feel so fucking brave with me? They might let you live, but I don't have any love toward you."

"Ian, now isn't the time," Jack says, using his boss voice. He reluctantly releases our father.

"You're lucky my men weren't allowed in this house. I've allowed your behavior to go unchecked because you're my son, but after this wedding, I will no longer consider you my son, Ian."

"Funny—when have you ever considered me your son?" That's true; they were always bumping heads since Ian was little. If my mother wasn't getting involved to stop them, I swear my father would have killed Ian.

"You were a terror and maybe you needed a lesson in respect, but I was no different with you than I was with any of you boys. If anything, I made you the tough bastard you are so that you could be the best enforcer we have." He whispers under his breath something that I'm about to kill him for.

"Please repeat that," I demanded.

"Your mother was more defective than I thought."

"What the fuck did you just say?"

"You better get the fuck out of here. I don't give a fuck if you have a vendetta against Saunders."

"No? Not even if I told you that he raped your mother and John's not my son? He's that bastard's child. He's the reason your mother is dead." My wife and I look at each other in horror.

"That's bullshit," I say, wanting to deny my father's claims because they're too damn outrageous.

"No? Test John and your bride. They're siblings." He smirks as he delivers that blow.

"You have to be kidding me. There's no way my father would do that."

"Are you kidding me? He's a piece of shit," my father adds.

"Are we really playing that game here?" Ian looks over at our father and nods his head up and down.

"Are you trying to tell me that my father somehow managed to take your mother and violate her, and you guys not only did nothing about it at the time, but haven't done anything about it all this time?"

She has a valid point. John is six now, and Saunders was still breathing. We look at my father, demanding answers.

"Well? What do you have to say to that?" Jack asks.

"You think I was going to share my embarrassment? She attended a charity function, and he had power over her. She was trapped and by the time I arrived, she was crying in a corner and there was nothing I could do."

"Where the fuck were her guards at?" Jack presses.

"They were kept outside of the party area so when she was grabbed, they were unaware. Why do you think I hate that bastard so much?" he challenged.

"And you did nothing about it all this time? Playing these petty wars with him and you didn't bother to tell us so we could take action this entire time." I didn't believe him.

"What makes you think John is his and not yours?" I questioned.

"I had him tested, but I never looked at the results. When your mother died, I just couldn't, and I destroyed them knowing that I'd raise him as my own son regardless because I owed it to her." I don't fucking believe him because the man's ego is bigger than his fat fucking head.

"If you were worried that he wasn't your son, why didn't you just have Mom get rid of the baby?" I ask. "She was too old to have another child, and it was a health risk as it was."

There is a disconcerting look on his face, and I already know the answer. He wanted to hold it against Saunders. "This is all about revenge, isn't it?"

"I just can't right now. I need some air." Claudia walks away toward the front door and opens it, but she's fucking crazy if she thinks this is over between us. Nothing changes our contract. If any of this is true, it only adds a little icing to the cake. I have my arm hooked around her waist and yank her back.

"Where the fuck do you think you're going?"

"Connor, I just can't. I need air."

"Excuse us." I led her outside toward the back. "Then I'll go with you, Wife."

"What? You don't trust me?"

"I don't trust your safety right now. I just learned that your father might have done something terrible to my mother. She was loved by everyone here. Do you know how many people would love to see revenge on him? You're a prime target. As my wife, you're protected, but I need to make everyone aware of it first." I pull her into my arms and hold her close.

"I've gotten mixed up in more than I can handle, Connor." God, sometimes her tenderness reminds me of my mother. Unfortunately, my mother was born into this, but luckily for Claudia, this marriage is temporary. She doesn't belong in this dark world, her delicate beauty and creativity suffocated by our violent darkness.

"Once we reach our goal, our marriage will crumble like many do during complicated times, and we can part ways."

"Good," she says with a hiccupped sob.

I hold her until she's calmed down and then we return to the house. The only one still there is Ian.

"Hey, everyone. I thought you guys could use some time alone, or rather, Jack demanded it. I'm just here to deliver the message. He said that dinner will be prepared at their house at seven to celebrate."

"Thank you, bro." Ian pulls me in for a hug.

"And you look beautiful, Claudia. Temporary or not, my brother is a lucky bastard." He leaves, and I know I'm right because she's a special woman and if circumstances were different, this might not have been a charade.

CHAPTER ELEVEN

CLAUDIA

IT'S BEEN HOURS SINCE OUR WEDDING, AND Connor has disappeared as if it isn't our wedding night. Not like it matters. He took me this morning and our marriage was a sham created on a twisted contract of vengeance, but that doesn't mean I want him out all night screwing other women. In fact, we had a deal. I swear, I'll rip his huge dick off.

I swiped my phone off his ass when he hugged me outside in the backyard. The fucker thought he was slick, but I noticed the pretty pink case sticking out of his pocket. He chuckled and said he wanted to keep track of my father's whereabouts so he didn't disturb the wedding. I understand that because it would have made it difficult too, but he could have just asked for it. Still, I locked the fucker and then tucked it away afterward.

Connor doesn't call me once while he's gone. No, he left me in his enormous house with at least two guards that I noticed and a hot young housekeeper in tight black yoga pants who has given me strange looks since I arrived.

I don't like her one bit. A gnawing feeling hits the pit of my stomach, and I wonder if he's banged her, and she's pissed because I'm here now. Right now, I can't worry about that because I'm scrolling through all my damn emails and messages. Ugh, it's insane how much stuff I have to do in the next few days. I hear the front door downstairs, and I wait for my piece-of-work husband to make it up here.

It's five in the morning, and Connor's finally strolling in. I try to contain my anger and the simmering jealousy that he's probably been out with someone else. He opens the bedroom door gingerly so as not to wake me, but I'm sitting in the chair by the window with my fingers steepled. "I need to go back to work, Connor. I have obligations that don't require just keeping my legs open only for you."

"Did you just say only for me? I'm your husband. Your legs are only open to me. Anyone else will be a dead motherfucker." His hand wraps around my throat and I'm off my feet, pinned to the bed in seconds. "Who the fuck do you think you'd run off to now that I popped that fucking cherry?" His eyes darken and his lips are firm. "Mirren?"

"I misspoke. I'm tired and grumpy because I'm all alone with nothing to do when I have a career that needs attention with less than two days left before the orders are due. Besides, so what if I said what I said? We're not really married, and you're not keeping to your vows."

He tugs on my hair, staring deep into my eyes with a deadly glare. My arousal is spinning all over my body.

"You're pushing it, Claudia. This fucking ring says it's real. Just because it's temporary doesn't mean it isn't real. As long as it's on your finger, neither of us is fucking anyone else. Do you understand? I work, so keep those claws tucked in. My hard dick might as well have your name tatted on it because it's yours." He rolls his hips, rubbing his length along my seam, causing my body to shake.

"I work too, and I have people counting on their orders being delivered."

"Look, I get that, but it's not like I can let you just go back to the bakery. They're watching and waiting for you."

"I have three orders pending and many more waiting for me to respond to them about my availability. Apparently, the pictures of you and I on the internet have created a stir."

"Plus, you have another cake to make."

"I haven't forgotten Nora's cake." I rolled my eyes at him.

"Get your attitude under control, or you're going to get spanked."

"You don't like when I roll my eyes, but I don't like when my husband disappears on my wedding night. It doesn't look real at all. No one will buy that we're married if you're out there working while I'm at home with your guards like a lonely little prisoner."

"Are you trying to insinuate something? Are you trying to get me to kill someone, Trouble?" He pulls out his gun and stands up.

"No. God, no. But what will others think?"

He sets his gun down on the nightstand and then slides his jacket off before quickly climbing on top of me. God, he smells so damn good, a mix of cologne and his natural masculine scent. "I don't give a fuck what others think. I'll fuck you in front of everyone and let them know you belong to me. Do you understand?" he growls in my ear. I'm so damn aroused. For some reason, I don't doubt him.

I moan, unable to use words when he touches me. "Claudia," he whispers, brushing his nose up and down my neck. "Did you miss me?"

"No," I huff.

"Yes, you did. Admit it and I'll get you all the equipment you need to work," he says, slipping a finger into my pussy.

"Bribery," I whimper, arching my hips.

"I never said anything about being a fair husband—only a faithful one." He bites down on my neck as he pushes two fingers inside and rubs his thumb over my clit. I splinter into pieces, coming apart for him, and I'm not sure I can be put back together. He's quick to slide off his clothes, taking me on the bed and pushing his thick, long length deep inside. I hold onto his strong biceps as he penetrates me.

"Admit it."

"I missed you."

"Good wife."

The devilish look in his icy blues goes straight to my core. "Fuck, I need this top off." He grabs my nightshirt and lifts it over my head. "Perfect." Connor licks his lips. His mouth crashes down on mine for a smooth kiss that I wasn't expecting.

Our chests brush against each other, and I feel his cock flex inside me. Now I understand why he was eager to get my top off. He wanted to feel me against him as much as I wanted it. Our kiss deepens, and I throw my arms around his neck. He growls and lifts me up like I weigh nothing, holding me on an angle he drives into me while he's still kissing me. He's sitting on his calves as I ride his lap, and then he sucks my nipple into his mouth and I throw my head back and cry out.

"Yes, my torment, come for me. Squeeze that beautifully tight pussy around my cock. Give me your screams before I fill you with my seed. You're lucky you can't get pregnant because I'm sure I would have knocked your pretty little ass up already." I run my fingers through his hair and scream, coming and thinking about a beautiful baby boy of his. He roars and fills me up.

"One day with my real husband," I sigh as he lays me on my back with his body over mine. He snarls and spanks my ass.

"Never mention another man to me again. I'll fuck that mouth so raw you won't be able to talk for a week." Oh my God—why am I turned on? My pussy flexes around his cock, and his eyes widen. "You want me to fuck that pretty, smart mouth of yours? Later. I'm tired, and I need a shower." He gets up and hits the shower while I roll over, too tired to move at the moment even though I need to move in a second.

———

CONNOR TAKES ME OVER TO VISIT NORA ALL DAY, which is fun, and we discuss her plans for her wedding cake. We have it marked down to the color and the flavor and the number of layers. I can't wait to get started.

Now, we're finally back at the house and just as we step over the threshold, his phone rings. It's Jack calling him for something, as if we didn't just leave. I feel like Connor is working nonstop. "Excuse me. I have to answer this, but there's something in the kitchen I want you to see."

I head into the kitchen. "Oh my goodness." My eyes widen comically when I see the transformation. What the hell did Connor do? He wasn't kidding about bribing me.

"Yes, the kitchen has been destroyed," his bitch of a housekeeper says.

"Destroyed?" I questioned, wondering how she could say that. I'm awed by the way it's been set up.

"Yes, it doesn't look like a home anymore," she remarks. For now, it's my home, so she needs to mind her own damn business.

I turn to her and smile brightly. "It's even better. There are two double ovens and a walk-in freezer. How did he do this so fast?"

"When Connor wants something done, he makes it happen." My hand glides over the smooth countertop.

"He certainly does. I love it," I sigh blissfully.

"You do?" he asks, entering the kitchen. I spin around and smile.

"It's perfect. I suppose bribery does work," I say, repeating our conversation from yesterday.

"You'll be able to get the work done, then?" he asks.

"Well, there are a lot of things I need, including ingredients, and I don't have a great deal of time to bake but if I have them, I should make things happen."

"Everything can be here in a couple of hours. I already have the pantry stocked with some of the things you had at your bakery."

"You did?" I run into his arms and throw myself onto him until I'm completely wrapped up around him. He holds me up as he chuckles deeply and then growls.

"Fuck, Trouble. Keep this up and I'm going to pin you to these nice clean counters and christen them," he whispers in my ear before nibbling on it. A bark comes from his side.

"Uh-oh. Someone else needs me too."

"I suppose I'll just have to enjoy my kitchen for a while by myself." He swats my ass and then I untangle myself from him.

"That's a good wife. Now, get to baking and let my housekeeper know what you need so she can get it for you." He kisses my lips and then says, "Come on, Cain. It's time for a walk." He leaves the kitchen, and then I take a long look around the room to see her glaring at me.

"I can't see what he sees in you," she whispers. I let it go and remind myself that she's just jealous. If I was her, I would be too. He and I are temporary, but he didn't even acknowledge her when he walked in the room.

"Do yourself a favor and find something to do while I check this out. If I need a list of things, I'll ask someone else. I don't trust you with anything." I narrow my eyes at her and then open the pantry to check the supplies. There is a large notepad against the door with a pen, and I make a list of things inside. After about half an hour, I'm only missing about ten baking items and they're not going to stop me from baking, but I'll need them before tomorrow night.

I set up the first round of cupcakes I need to bake. It's a two-dozen cream-filled chocolate birthday order. Most of the supplies are new, including all the rolling pins, mixing bowls, and baking sheets.

Forty minutes later, I'm done with the first two orders on my list, which is freaking amazing. "Trouble, how is it going?" he asks as he comes into the kitchen. God, he looks so sexy in just a nicely tailored dress shirt and his sleeves rolled up his forearms.

"Good. I'm almost done. I have a list of things I need, and actually, I need to add a few more."

"Where is my housekeeper? I can have her get them."

"Isn't there anyone else you can send to do it?"

"Um…is there something wrong with her?" he asked me.

I hated how jealous this came off as, but the bitch hated me more than I hated her and I really couldn't stomach her. "I don't want to rely on someone you used to…"

"You think I fucked her?" He lets out a chuckle and shakes his head. "Sweetheart. Not in a million years. I have rules about things like that, and I wouldn't disrespect you like that." He moves around the counter and then slides his arms around my waist. "Kiss me right now before I spank you."

"Why?"

"Because I said so."

"You're lucky I'm in a good mood." I press my lips to his and then pull back, giving him a chaste kiss.

"You better try again, Wife. I'm about to spank that pretty round ass until it's red," he says, staring at me. He cups my ass and rubs my pussy up against his hard length. I moan and then kiss him properly.

"Are you done for the night?"

"I have to put all this away and turn everything off." I set the cupcakes to cool in the freezer, and then I turn all the ovens off.

"Let's go upstairs, and then you can properly thank me for the mini-bakery."

"How would you like my thanks?" I questioned, my lips parting softly while I run my hand over his chest all the way down to the edge of his belt.

He takes my hand and sets it over his hard cock. "On your knees, for starters." I blush, not because I'm embarrassed. I'm excited. Smiling, I dart out of the kitchen in a mad dash up to our bedroom. He follows, taking the steps two at a time.

I find myself on my knees, taking his length to the back of my throat until he roars my name, filling my mouth. Then he proceeds to spend the evening licking, eating, and then fucking me until I pass out. I'm not trouble, I'm in trouble.

CHAPTER TWELVE

CONNOR

THE PAST TWO DAYS I WAS ABLE TO AVOID THE asshole governor and the attorney general, but today won't be my lucky day. I'm in the middle of the city on business, and I'm immediately confronted by the two pricks as I pull up to the state building for a meeting with my investors. Of course, I knew it would happen, and my lawyer is waiting in the wings due to the fact that the bastards can't be trusted.

"Well, well, well. If it isn't my new father-in-law. It's pretty nice to see you," I say. The color on his face disappears, turning his red cheeks completely pale. "Oh, did you not see the notice? Claudia and I are married. It was a private ceremony with our family."

"You bastard." He lunges for me, but his men are quick to pull him back before he creates a scene in front of the press, who have their cameras flashing.

"You don't look so devastated, Mirren. I guess Claudia wasn't that special."

"Pussy is pussy. Once you've had it, why marry it?" he says, trying to set me off, but it's not going to work. The fucking idiot never touched her, and I know it.

"Why are you trying to goad me, Mirren? I know you didn't stick your diseased dick anywhere near my wife, so it won't work. I got her sweet cherry on our wedding day."

"Now, if you two will excuse me, I have business to attend to that you're delaying me for. If you two come for me or my wife again, I'll have you arrested, Mirren. Here is the restraining order I had filed from the lovely text messages you sent her. Enjoy."

I walk away and then I turn around, walk up to the governor, and whisper so only he can hear me, "Oh, yeah, and one more thing, Saunders. I've heard a nasty rumor that you raped my mother. If that's true, I will make sure you're a dead man walking."

He shakes his head, and his jaw becomes slack. "That's a filthy lie. Your father has a lot of dirty secrets that he's kept from you boys, and what happened between Evelyn and I...is not open for discussion. Your mother deserved better than your father and me." He sighed, shaking his head. Did the man just actually show a sign of remorse? Something he clearly didn't have for my wife.

I can't sit through the fucking meeting because the look on Saunders's face was real. He was shocked by the allegation, and I could read liars like him. He is a professional, but this is legitimate.

He might not have raped her, but something else happened that he doesn't want to talk about. My father and I need to have a talk, but I need to speak with Jack first before I bust down my father's door.

The meeting ends earlier than it needs to because I have no patience. "O'Neill, handle this shit. I have other matters to deal with. Excuse me."

I'm out of there and on the street before an hour passes. My phone in hand, I have my brother's number ringing. "Jack, we need to talk. Where are you?"

"I'm at my office in the city."

"I'm on my way there now." I end the call right away and then tell my driver to take me to my brother's office. I'm itching for a fight, and I'm about to pound someone's face in. As I'm about ready to lose it, my phone rings. I look at the screen, and my sexy wife's image pops up on it. Fuck me. The tension slips away from my shoulders. "What's up, Trouble?"

"I was wondering if I had someone who could take me to make these deliveries."

"I'll have Johnny take you," I say. I'd love to be the one to take her, but there are just too many things going on and frankly, I'm not in the right headspace to be nice to strangers.

"Okay. Thank you. I hope you have a good day."

"It's better now. I'll see you later." That's the truth too.

"Okay." She ends the call, and my chest feels lighter, even for a brief moment. We pull up to my brother's office building, and my temper is back.

"Park in the garage. I'll let you know when I'm ready." He nods and I leave the vehicle, walking up to the main entrance of the Chicago skyscraper. The security at the desk smiles and waves me off as soon as he sees me.

"Good morning, Mr. MacNamara."

"Good morning, Phil."

As soon as I enter my brother's office, he closes the door behind me and hisses, "So, Connor, what's going on?"

I run my fingers through my short hair, wanting to tug at it. "Bro, I just confronted Mirren and the governor. The piece of shit had a relationship with Mom of some sort. I have no idea what happened between them, or if either he or Dad are telling the truth. But he called Dad a liar and said I needed to get the truth out of him. He was adamant that he didn't violate Mom, but that she deserved better than both of them."

"I don't trust either of them." He paces and then falls back in his office chair and rubs his face.

"What's going on with the DNA test?"

"I have them running it at a special lab. It should be here any minute. In fact, I'll call my guy and find out." I sit down in front of his desk while he makes the call. "Hey, Reginald. What do you have for me? Are the results in?"

"Oh, I was just about to call you. Sorry—I was on lunch. Give me one minute and I'll get the report," he garbles with a mouth full of food. "It looks like...I'm sorry, but John is your half-brother. You share the same mother, but you don't share the same father together. The female DNA is unrelated."

"Thank you. Please send over the report," Jack says before ending the call.

"Fuck." We both know what this means. My mother had been with a different man than Saunders.

"So, what do you think happened?" I asked.

"I don't know. I went to look to see if Mom attended a charity event with the governor, and I found one around the time that John would have been conceived," Jack informed me. He paused and then took a deep breath before he added, "The thing is, Dad wasn't in town. He happened to be in Europe. So, Dad's story isn't quite true."

"Not quite, but it doesn't change everything. Mom could have waited to tell him, or someone else could have rescued her, like her guards. We need to find answers."

So, Saunders isn't the one who knocked Mom up, and that means Dad's hatred for him is for nothing.

It's time to sit my father down. We drove to the estate and immediately went to his residence. Jack and I confront him in his study, and he looks petrified. "Dad, you weren't being honest with us, and we want fucking answers right now," Jack snarls, slamming him back onto the sofa by his shoulder. "Saunders is not John's dad, and neither are you."

"What was going on with you and Mom?" I add.

"That's not right. That can't be. She was having an affair with him. That bastard belonged to Saunders for sure."

"Did you just call John a bastard?"

"Well, isn't he? He's not my kid."

"If you knew you weren't the father, then why did you force Mom to have the baby?" I ask. He didn't give us a good excuse last time, but we need answers now.

"Because she fucking betrayed me. She had an affair with that bastard. I wanted his head, and I wanted her to pay for what she did. And she paid, all right, with her fucking life." I punched him dead in the face, hearing the crunch and breaking his nose.

He shouts, but neither of us care. Jack continues, "I can't believe Mom was cheating on you. She never left the house, so there was no way she had a chance."

"Oh, she had a chance, all right. With all her fucking charity work, that's how she met the bastard." I try to think about all the times my mom was out, and I would say that there were a fair few over the years, but honestly we were working so much we didn't know, and so was our father. There is a good chance he's telling the truth about this.

This still doesn't explain why he isn't John's father, if she was having an affair with him.

"Did you test his DNA? Or did you just test your wife and John? Maybe his wife was a whore too," he stated like he has no damn self-preservation.

"Watch what you fucking say about my mother, because I'm one step from choking the life out of you," Jack roars, holding onto the edge of my father's chair like he's tempted to end him.

"Whatever Mom did, it didn't change the fact that you were a bastard too. Like you didn't have affair after affair," I reminded him.

"That's different. Like you can see, she had a child that didn't belong to me," he snorted in disgust.

"Yeah, well, how many other siblings do we have that none of us know about?" I asked.

"None, because I was fucking smart about it."

"Are you sure?" Jack questioned.

"Positive." He nods. "I got fixed before John was conceived." So that's how he was sure John wasn't his.

"Why would you do that? It's a little crazy at your age unless you have a reason."

"One of my whores ended up pregnant, and I took care of it. Made sure it wouldn't happen again. So, you don't have any other siblings. Now, if you're fucking done, could you give me a towel or let me take care of my fucking face?"

I walk over to the mini bar and grab a towel, tossing it at him. "Now what are we going to do? You fucking lied to us and told us that he raped her. I could have fucking shot him right in the head in front of everybody in downtown Chicago."

"Not my problem that you're a damn hot head," he scoffs.

"Do you even hear yourself sometimes? You raised us, you idiot. You goaded us into believing something ridiculously evil about a man who already hates us."

"I'm going to go talk to Saunders again and get some answers, unless you're willing to give me the fucking truth. The whole damn truth. And don't play *A Few Good Men* with me and tell me I can't handle it."

"I gave you the truth." I can't believe a word out of his mouth.

"Bullshit."

I have so many damn questions, and no damn answers. "Look, I don't have time for this shit. My wife is calling me, and honestly, I'd rather be getting some pussy instead of here talking to you, playing the circle game," I say, even though my phone isn't ringing. Being with Claudia makes my motherfucking day and it's better than anything else here.

"Are you coming, Jack?"

"Yep, right behind you." Jack can't stop glaring at my father, even as we start walking away.

We both leave, and as we're leaving, I get a sinking feeling some shit is about to go down. Still, all I want to do is go home and slip my dick in that bad-ass woman in our home.

I can smell that she's in the kitchen and as I enter, my teeth are on edge.

CHAPTER THIRTEEN

CLAUDIA

"I love you, Nicky. Talk to you later. Bye." I realize my mistake as the pressure changes in the room. It's as if I can feel him anytime he's nearby. I lift my head to the side and see the darkness in his eyes. His light blues seem to disappear around his dark lashes and pupils. There's no doubt he misinterpreted my call, but I know there's no way he's going to listen right now. There's that hungry look in his predatory gaze. I see the determination to prove a point to me. A shiver of both fear and excitement fills me up.

"I know my fucking ears didn't just deceive me. First, I came home to find you half naked walking around my house with my men all around as if you're a goddamn stripper. Now, you're chatting with your ex-fiancé, reminding him how much you love him. What the fuck am I going to do with you?" His voice is deep, hostile as he stares at me.

"It's not like that," I insist, trying to explain, but he shakes his head and stalks toward me with a domineering gaze.

"Don't lie to me. The apple doesn't fall too far from the motherfucking tree."

"No, it doesn't. Remember that—your father isn't any better than mine. You're the one who's been gone, and then you have the nerve to come and accuse me of things." I slam my hand against my hip.

"It's not hard, sweetheart, when I can hear them coming from your pretty, deceitful lips."

I glare at him, getting in his angry, possessive face. "Nicky is a four-year-old boy, jackass, and it's his birthday tomorrow. I was finishing up his order that would have been done already if it wasn't for your foolish demands that I live here instead of back at my apartment—above my bakery."

His tone shifts just a bit at the revelation, but his hunger to prove a point is still in his eyes. "Foolish? Do you think your safety is foolish? You forget why you came to me."

"I think we're both forgetting why," I reminded him.

"It's not time yet, little girl. I told you I'll have to wait until Jack and Nora's wedding is over. I'm not ruining that shit for them. It's bad enough your father tried to destroy it. They've been through enough. Now, are you done running that smart mouth of yours, because you need a lesson."

"A lesson?" I tilt my head and stare up at my husband who has left no room between us now.

"Yes."

"In what?"

"In how to behave and act like you actually belong to me. I need to remind these men that you're mine. Do you want me to fuck you in front of all of them?" My face flushes, and I try to hide the desire washing through me for him to take me in front of everyone.

"It's only temporary, remember? A fake marriage," I stammer out, biting my bottom lip.

"Temporary or not, everyone has to fucking believe it to keep your little stubborn ass protected. I'm starting to wonder if you don't want this to work."

"You know I do."

"Then act like the obedient wife." He squeezes my pussy, knowing I'm soaked.

"I'll consider it."

"Consider this." He looks at the items on the counter. "I'm going to have to give everyone a show of what's mine, even if it's temporary. They don't know about our arrangement. All they know is your mine and that tight pussy, smart mouth, sexy, plump breasts, and juicy, firm ass belong to me."

"You wouldn't."

"Are you challenging me? Because I'm always up for a challenge. I think you are too. This soaked pussy clenching against my fingers wants to be fucked like a good wife in front of everyone. You want them to know you belong to me, don't you?" He bites my neck. "Answer me, Claudia."

"Yes," I cry out.

"Good."

"Oh, look." He picks up the small jar of coconut oil and reads the label. "What could we do with this coconut oil?" He sets it back on the counter then calmly says, "Lean forward, Claudia. I'm about to teach you a lesson when it comes to walking around the house in just my dress shirt and panties, looking too damn delectable for anyone to see. You're my wife."

"Temporarily," I reminded him again. "Besides, your shirt fits like a dress."

"I don't care if it does. It's the visual it presents. And I haven't forgotten it's temporary, but every time you correct me, I think I'll punish you."

He swats my panty covered ass. "Ouch."

His fingers dip into the coconut oil, moves my underwear to the side, and then he slips one digit into my backside. The feeling is strange but good. "Behave, my little submissive one."

"Fuck," I stammer as he goes deeper, pushing in and then pulling out.

"This puckered hole is getting nice and lubed for me," he grunts. "I can't wait until I'm balls deep in there and you're bouncing on it like you're doing with my fingers. You like getting your ass fucked. Let's see how far we can go. What do we have here?" He runs his hand over the small fondant roller, and my mind immediately goes to exactly where his brain goes.

"Connor, what are you doing with that?" I asked.

"I wonder what you'd do if I slipped this inside."

"That's too big," I argued. It's definitely too stiff.

"It's not bigger than me."

"It's for rolling fondant."

"I'll buy you a replacement." He grabs the coconut oil and coats the fondant roller. I don't stop him as he slowly slides it between my cheeks. "I don't have anything to train your ass. My dick is a lot fatter than this fucker, and I need to teach my sexy wife that you're mine."

"I understand."

"Do you? Because you're walking around here half fucking naked. Pussy begging to be taken by anyone who would be bold enough to defy me. Hell, do you know what I'd do to them for even touching what belongs to me?" He rubs the round edge of the roller against my hole and presses inward. I gasp and moan as he glides it in. "So damn easy.

You're a very good girl for me. I can't wait to stuff my fat dick inside your ass," he growls against my ear.

"Connor," I moan, holding on to the counter, leaning forward so my tits are pressed against the surface. I'm glad I have the shirt on because the counter is cool. It's a lot of pressure, but my pussy clenches with excitement thinking of his dick taking me from behind. "Fuck me."

"You want me to fuck that ass?" he asks, but it comes out more as a command.

My entire body shivers with excitement. "Yes, I want to feel you in me. Dominate me."

He pulls the roller from my ass and tosses it in the trash. "First, come here." He leads me into the living room. "Men, my wife isn't for your consumption. If I catch any of you putting your hands on her, I'll chop them off, and then next will be your cocks, understood?"

"Yes," they answer.

"Knees, Wife." I lower myself and watch as he frees himself. God, I'm so damn wet. Is he going to fuck me in front of everyone? I'm going to come so fast. "Give me your mouth," he says, dropping his head for a deep kiss. He pulls off gently and then lines up his cock, sliding it into my mouth. I'm practically starving for him. I roll my tongue around his length before taking the head into my throat, going deeper inch by inch. Connor's cock is huge, and I gag about halfway down and have to pull back and go back down. I'm bobbing like a pro after a few seconds, taking more and more until he snarls, "Enough."

He lifts me to my feet and then sits down. He summons me to straddle him. I still have my shirt on so they can't see anything but my thighs as he pushes me down his thick pole, impaling me.

I can hear the groans around the room. We both know they're getting aroused by the show. Several of the men leave, but those who stay are getting an education on making a woman come. Because Connor does everything to please me. Every stroke, touch, and kiss are meant to bring me to orgasm.

I bounce on his thick cock until I'm screaming his name.

"Leave us." Everyone leaves and he picks me up, carrying me to our bedroom.

"Are you okay?" I ask him.

"That's about as much as I could tolerate. Lose the top and get on all fours. I'm not done with you. I let them see what's mine. I need to remind you that you're only mine," he snarls. There's a jealous tone and I'm loving it.

I quickly lose my top and get into position. My naked body is posed for him with my ass up in the air. When I turn my head to look at him, he's down to just his boxer briefs. "Oh my goodness, Connor, you're so hot."

"Thank you, Trouble, but it's nothing compared to you." He slides the last bit of material down, and his huge cock that was buried deep in me moments ago is gloriously hard and ready to be in me again. I lick my lips ready to suck every drop of cum out of him, but right now he has other plans.

"Time to fill that new little hole." My pussy clenches, and I moan with excitement. "Fuck, I love your enthusiasm." He swats my ass as he climbs up behind me. His hands caress my round cheeks, giving them attention before he slips two fingers into my pussy. I gasp. "Don't start coming too soon."

"Don't tell me what to do."

He spanks me with the other hand. "I always tell you what to do. I will fuck you how I please, and you will come like a fucking good girl because you love it." My body responds, gushing juices all over his fingers. "That's right. You know who is in charge. Now, behave because my dick is a lot bigger than that thing and I don't want to hurt your little hole."

"Okay." I relax as he pushes his wet fingers into my ass, stretching me as much as he can. His cock slips into my pussy, and I'm fighting my orgasm. Damn the man.

He leans over me, sending his cock deeper into my pussy and whispers, "I said don't come."

"I'm not," I squeal, trying to resist, but the man makes me feel so good, so protected and owned.

"But you want to come," he chuckles.

"Stop fucking me so damn good," I challenged him.

"Never," he replies, biting my ear.

He quickly pulls out of both holes, and then his big tip presses at my back entrance. I relax and trust that he'll please me. "Good girl," he whispers. Inch by inch, he pushes past each ring. It stings, but there's enough lube from the coconut oil and my juices that he fits perfectly.

He wraps his hand around my throat. "Fuck, you're taking me so damn well. I love the way you take my huge cock in your tiny hole. Do you like me fucking that little slot?"

"Yes," I answered.

He grunts and moves in and out, nearly pulling completely out of me before thrusting back in. I gasp each time. My body is being used and I love it. He wraps one hand around my waist as he lifts my upper body off the bed, pumping into me. "You feel incredible and I'm going to come. Come for me, Claudia," he growls. He lowers his hand and strums my clit. I didn't realize how close I was, and I shot off, coming again. He roars and floods my rear. When he pulls out, the rest is on my ass.

"Fuck. You are trouble, Claudia." He kisses my lips and then growls. "We need a shower. Maybe two, because I have a feeling we're going to get dirty again." He scoops me up and takes me to the bathroom. Damn it, he's the one who is trouble.

We'd barely rinsed off when his phone rang. He pressed his forehead to mine. "Sorry, sexy. This might be important." He steps out of the bathroom in all his glory and answers the call. The way his body tenses, I know our interlude has just ended.

"I have to go."

"Just be careful."

"I will." He kisses me hard and quickly gets dressed while I close myself in the bathroom, trying to stop these feelings I'm having. "Damn it, Claudia. No falling for your temporary husband."

CHAPTER FOURTEEN

CONNOR

My phone buzzes, and it's a tip on Espinoza. As soon as I'm off the phone, I kiss Claudia and get dressed because it's back to business and this is some serious family business. I'm at Jack's house within ten minutes after the call, barging through the door. Unlike him, I don't have a kid, interrupting my sexy times, so the poor guy didn't get Nora alone.

"What's up, Con?"

"Looks like we got a lead," I tell him.

"Are you serious? The son of a bitch has finally been found?" my brother asks.

"Looks like it. Fieri is taking him to our spot," I add with a grin. I can't wait to get my damn hands on that piece of shit.

"Well, it looks like our women will have to wait," he grumbles. I don't tell him that I've already got my hands on Claudia more than once, but it's never enough.

As much as I hate it, he's right. I love having my hands on Claudia, but this is so damn important. Besides, she understood that my business came first especially since she reminded me so often how temporary we were. "Damn it." That constantly hits like a ton of bricks in my chest, but I'm refusing to evaluate it.

"Time to chop up that bastard for good and get some answers," Jack snarls, jumping in the passenger seat since I drove my SUV over.

I rub my hands together, grinning from ear to ear. "Let's roll."

We drove to our Northside den of torture and met with Fieri. "Well, hello, my future brother-in-law," Jack says, greeting him.

"I'm annoyed that you're already not married to my sister. It feels like an insult that you're shacking up with her."

"As you know, the wedding will happen as soon as we wrap up all this bullshit." If he's trying to pick a fight with Jack, now isn't the time. Then again, knowing that I'm married and it took all of minutes to do, must rankle Fieri's nerves.

"I know, I know. That's why I found this prick for you and wrapped him up in a pretty bow." We walk into the main room and there he is, literally tied up with a fucking red bow on his head. I do my best not to laugh, but that shit is fucking hysterical.

"Why, thank you for the wedding present, Fieri," Jack says.

"My pleasure. Don't say I never gave you anything." He chuckles. I walk around Espinosa and snarl and growl like a damn wild animal. We have no intention of killing him so quickly. I need answers, and we're not leaving until he gives them to us.

I rush him, and he flinches like a scared little bitch, so much so he nearly sends his chair falling onto the floor, but one of the men catches it. "Thanks for the save. I can't have him busting his head before I get answers."

"Please spare me, and I'll tell you what you want to know," he pleads like they always do.

"There's nothing you could tell us that would spare your life."

"I didn't orchestrate the kidnapping, and my sister tried to do the right thing. She was murdered to protect his secret."

"Whose secret?"

"The secret of who really set it up." My gut tells me who it was, and from the look on Jack's face, he knows it too. The one who fucking pulled the damn trigger. The only person who had a motive to get rid of John in the first place.

"Go on."

"Your father." We both glare at him and before we can speak, he blurts out more. "I have proof that your father was in on your brother's kidnapping."

"Go on. Tell us."

"I want to live."

"Why would we do that when you tried to kill me and have me framed?"

"I just wanted to survive. Your father is evil."

"What's your motherfucking proof?"

"I have it on file. All our meetings. He doesn't know that I recorded them. My sister kept records too, but they went up in her house with your men who tried to find John. I was only there to kill that fucker because I wanted to get revenge for my sister. Do you have any idea how deep we were when this happened? My sister loved that boy, and for what? She lost her life to protect him. I never wanted anything bad to happen to him, but everyone else could burn. Hurting a kid had never been in my plans either. Your dad was the one who wanted him gone, permanently."

"A word, Connor."

Jack and I take a step away. "What are you thinking?" I ask him.

"Dad never gave his sister a chance. She deserved to live, and he took her life."

"Yeah, but this fucker helped kill so many of our men."

"And he killed our enemies too. If he leads us to the truth, I'm willing to send him off as payment for his sister." I nod.

We return back to a tied-up Espinosa. "The evidence?"

"It's in my bag. I always carry a copy on me and in a secret spot in a locker." Fieri grabs his bag and digs through it until he finds the small device.

"This better not be a fucking game because this will determine if we set you free."

"It's not. I swear. I want your fucking son-of-a-bitch father to pay for what he's done. My sister shouldn't have died just because she wanted your brother to live."

"No, she shouldn't have. If she had lived, I would have found my brother and my future wife a long time ago."

Fieri plays the tape, and on it, my father's voice can be heard with that piece-of-shit Giles working out a plan to kidnap my brother. *"I don't just want him kidnapped, I want him found dead in a ditch somewhere. Of course, I want you to make it look real and like a ransom. We'll put it on the damn Fieri family. They've been on my list for far too fucking long. I can't put it on Saunders like I'd like to because that fuck wouldn't harm John."*

"What about your other boys?"

"Not when they're around. One, they're my heirs, and two, they're deadly and you might not make it out alive."

"I've heard everything I need to," Jack says. Fieri ends it.

"Espinosa, you have one opportunity to redeem yourself. I don't ever want to see your face again. You need to skip town and stay gone because I can't trust your motives. Anyone that works with my father can't be trusted."

His eyes are shocked wide open. A newfound sense of relief. "I understand. I understand. I won't let you down. Thank you for another chance." He bends and nods, thanking us several times.

"Take him to a secured area and let him go," Jack tells Johnny, and then we take the evidence and stare at each other.

Jack cracks his knuckles, looking at me without actually seeing me. "We need to decide how we deal with our father." I understood exactly how he was feeling. We'd been betrayed by him without a doubt. We'd always believed he was guilty and yet we let him talk his way out of it, and allowed ourselves to be blinded by familial loyalty and fear of the other families noticing the unrest and capitalizing on it.

"Yes, we do." I want to put a bullet in his head. He hadn't truly cared about any of us. We were all a means to an end. He'd forgotten all about family when it came to his own personal happiness and success.

Vince comes into the vacant room in a mad dash. "Sir, there's a fire at the estate."

"What?"

"Sorry, I know the signal's jammed in here, but the alert came on." We ran out of the property, and I immediately regret letting Espinosa go.

We hop into my SUV, and I say, "Call Claudia."

The Bluetooth on the dash dials my wife's number, and she answers. "Connor, they're moving us to a secure area. What's going on?"

"There's a fire on the estate. Where are you?" I asked, wanting to find her as soon as possible.

"I was at Nora's when things went crazy."

"Okay. So you're all safe?" I asked.

"Yes. I just got back from delivering the cupcakes when Ian arrived and your father left."

"He left?" The fucking bastard knew we were coming.

"Yes."

"Baby, is Ian there?" I asked gently.

"Yes. He's right here."

"Put him on the phone." She handed the phone over.

"Ian. What the hell is going on?"

"It's Dad's garage. It caught fire, and the fire department is on the way. I'm just making sure the women are safe until it's all clear." A loud boom goes off in the background.

"Fuck."

"What the hell was that?" I roar.

Jack answers, "Dad's house." He can see the cameras on his phone, so he's checking the surveillance.

"The bastard."

"Keep our families protected," I say.

"I will."

"We're on our way, and we need to talk to you." The entire time my mind is on getting back to the house. Jack rode in with me, so we're riding back together, so I can see the stress in his voice.

"Put Nora on the phone. Jack wants to talk to her." He talks to Nora to see how she and John are doing, but I'm not focused on their conversation since my mind is reeling with thoughts of murder. If Espinosa has anything to do with this, he's a dead man.

"Okay," Jack says, and then ends the call.

Just then Jack gets a call from Johnny and then it quickly ends.

He looks at me and purses his lips. "Dad got a tip that we had Espinosa. I suppose they didn't think it was meant to be kept a secret. The men cheered and when he learned of it, he tucked his tail between his legs and ran."

"Fucker." I shake my head in wonder. "So, the fire?"

"I wonder what he was hiding in that house. What motherfucking secrets are in there?"

"I don't know, but whatever they are, he obviously didn't want us to find them, so he'd rather burn everything to the ground." I hope we can find something even though it's burned to a crisp.

"Fucking prick." My head is spinning with this news. I don't have time for this shit. By the time we pull up to the gates, five trucks are there putting out the blaze. My security is still at the gates, but they are open, which sets my teeth on edge. Jack also notes the problem.

"Do you think this is a setup?"

"I don't know, but we're going to watch the cameras from the time the blaze started until they leave and if anyone sneaks in, they'll be fucking shot."

"Has anyone passed through?"

"Not that we noticed, but there have been a few sketchy moments. We've been a bit preoccupied with the blaze and the emergency vehicles."

"We understand. Watch the cameras and pay attention, because it could go south at any second," Jack explained. We pull away from the security station and then he looks at me. "I don't give a fuck about the fire, Connor. I need to see my family."

"Same here."

We drove to his house and went inside. Immediately our women jump into our arms. "I missed you, too," I tease her, but it's the fucking truth.

"Shut up." She slapped my chest.

"I was worried about an attack. Ian told me there was nothing to worry about, but it doesn't mean that he wasn't just placating me."

"True," Ian admits, smirking.

"Ladies, can you please play with John somewhere safe while we speak to Ian privately?" Jack asks. I give Claudia a pleading look, hoping that she doesn't put up a fight.

"Is this about my father?" she asked, brow raising.

"No. It's not. Fuck, I completely forgot about him," Jack says.

"Me too." A lot has happened since I ran into that prick this morning. It's so damn messed up that we each have a fucked-up parent.

The ladies lead John away and once they're safely out of listening range, Ian asks, "What the hell is going on? You two are acting weird."

"Dad set the house on fire, and he fled."

"What do you fucking mean?"

"He's the one who orchestrated John's kidnapping, and he planned to have him killed. If it wasn't for the nanny, they would have executed John."

"I'll destroy him." Ian flexes his fists, clenching them tightly while he grinds his teeth. I know he's about ready for war, which is why I didn't mention the situation in front of the women. He could lose his shit and smash something and startle them.

"We need to get rid of the police and firefighters, but why don't we just track the fuck?"

"Good idea, Connor." My brother pulls up an app and runs the tracker on the car our father took. It's traced to only two miles outside the damn estate.

"We need to approach this vehicle cautiously, if there is even a vehicle there. He could have found the tracker and tossed it." They nod, and then we leave his office and find the women sitting around the living room with John, playing with his toys. "We need to speak with the fire department and then the police."

"I'm going to head out and check the car, okay?" Ian offers.

"Please do, but be careful because I don't trust our father, especially when it comes to you. He wouldn't waste an opportunity to take you out," Jack says.

"No doubt. The bastard would definitely try to get me. Connor, you want to go instead?"

I chuckle. "Sure." We leave the house and drive toward my father's just as the firefighters finally put out the blaze.

"They are the owners," Johnny informs a man in uniform, pointing directly at us as we step out of my SUV.

"Boss, this is Chief Moses. He has information about the fire and was looking for you." Jack shakes his hand and then so do Ian and I.

"Okay. Please let us know what is happening with our father's home."

"Unfortunately, there was a major accelerant used in the garage. It wasn't just in a container that could be explained away. Although it's natural to have corrosive and explosive-type items in the garage, this was different. The house caught fire afterward, and inside there were two bombs—inside the main door to the garage, and the other in the kitchen. The mansion is mostly destroyed. We found two dead bodies inside so far."

The color leaves our face. He didn't even have the decency to send them off before he set the place ablaze—the damn devil. Damn it, the man was getting desperate and that meant even more dangerous than we had already thought.

"You're going to need to find my father," I say.

"We believe he was one of the people in the fire."

"What?" Jack, Ian, and I stare at each other in shock. They saw his vehicle leave, and so did our guys. It wasn't him. Who did he set up inside the house?

"Can we see the body?" Jack asks first. We all want to know if they really have the old man. There is no way in hell we believe it.

"They were badly burned and removed to the medical examiner's office. You'll have to meet with them."

"Thank you. If you'll excuse us, we need to return to our family. How much longer will they all be here?" He gives Jack a peculiar look, but I suppose it's because we don't care if our father's dead or not.

"The fire is out, but the smoke is unfortunately strong. Please keep indoors, and if anyone has breathing problems, make sure they're away from this."

"We will. Thank you again." We each shake his hand again and then drive back to Jack's. "Do you think Saunders has anything to do with this?"

"No, I believe this is all Dad. I need to figure out what to do with Saunders. With all this damn attention Dad's just drawn on us, I can't just have Saunders killed because it would be like a fucking neon sign pointed right at me."

"You're right."

"But delaying it will piss off Claudia."

"She knows you're waiting until after my wedding, so at least that gives you another week."

"Yeah, but with dad's death," I say with air quotes. "You'll be expected to postpone it."

"The fuck I am. Nora and I are getting married next week, and your wife is going to make a killer cake that Nora has been dreaming about for days."

"Fine with me."

"You'll get no complaints from me. I love cake, and if you're married, the other families will find you stronger. That means the head of the family will usher in his future family," Ian says.

"Since when do you care about the other families?" I ask Ian.

"I don't, but going to war with other pricks isn't something I want. Any sense of weakness, and we'll have a problem. You know that as much as I do. By the way, I've got to go. I'll check the damn car, but I'm guessing the car wasn't there and he tossed the tracker out on the road."

"Okay. Just be careful and call us," Jack tells him, but Ian just nods. He's always such a damn hard head.

"Let's go in and see our wives."

"Your old room is still available," Jack says.

"Thanks. I don't know if I feel like waiting until I get home. She might get her first ride in the car."

He chuckled, and we entered the house. "Trouble, where are you?" Whatever the plans are, I need to be inside her so I can think straight again.

She pops into the foyer with a smile. I open my arms, and she jumps into them. "Not in my foyer," Jack calls out. I chuckle and carry her upstairs to the bedroom I use whenever I stay over.

We fuck fast and hungrily. "Connor," she moans, taking my dick deep. I didn't even bother to take all my clothes off because I needed to be inside my wife.

"Mine," I growled, pumping into her. Our movements are intense, rocking the bed, our headboard banging against the wall.

"Fuck, I'm coming," Claudia shouts. I grip her hips and come inside her. A dark thought enters my mind, and I want her pregnant. I shake that off because we're only temporary, and I know it. It's what she wants, and it's what I promised. Pressing my head to her shoulder, I catch my breath.

"Damn you're going to kill me with your perfect body," I grunt, sliding my cock in and out twice before pulling away.

"You're the killer. That damn thing is dangerous." She sighs, throwing her arms above her head, so relaxed. I see my seed dripping out, and I reach between her thighs and push that shit back inside. She moans and parts her thighs for me. Something about it turns me on, and I climb back on her.

"Round two."

"Damn right. When I want you, I fuck you. You understand me?" I grip her throat, holding her roughly as I fuck her hole again.

"Yes, Husband."

"Good girl." I take her again, but this time it's a little slower and I lose myself inside her body. This time when I come, I quickly get up because this is all wrong. I take a fast shower and when I come out, Claudia is passed out on the bed.

Being inside Claudia always feels right. But after this moment, something just feels wrong, and I can't put my finger on it. It isn't her, or us, for that matter. Just my gut feeling that something bad is happening. My phone rings, and I know I'm right. We were down the hall, but my brother is calling me anyway. "What's up, Jack?"

"I haven't heard from Ian yet. He was supposed to get back to me about the car. That was over an hour ago."

"Shit. I'm on my way there."

"I've already sent a guy over there right now. Meet me downstairs." I stare at my wife and know that I can't tell her a damn thing, but I have to go. "Hold on. I have Mel on the other line." He includes him on the call.

"Boss, I called the ambulance. It's bad. Ian's been shot multiple times. He looks like he's been ambushed." My heart fucking sinks.

"Son of a bitch. Okay, thanks for that. We will be there in a second."

I hang up and rush out of the room, leaving Claudia sleeping in bed. I race down the stairs faster than I ever have before. We don't explain to anyone as we burst out of the house.

Jack and I rush over to the scene without giving our women any explanation because we can't speak or waste time. When we arrive, Ian's unresponsive as they work on him. There's nothing we can do, and they don't let us get close. The ambulance is just putting my brother in the back when I tell a shaken Jack to get himself together. "Jack, bundle up our family. I'm riding with Ian." He nods, wiping the tears from his eyes. I trust him with my wife, and he needs to protect his family, so I know he'll want to be with them.

I hop in back, and the medics are working quickly on my brother. "We're ready. Hang in there, Ian," the medic says.

I stare at my little brother with my heart in my throat. The blood is all over his handsome face. Of all of us, he got the best looks. I always thought that, and he used to rub it in our faces that he had the best hair too. We knew that we shouldn't have sent him out there by himself. "Damn it, Ian. You better not die."

My little brother still isn't responsive as they work on him. His pulse is weak and thready as they tend to his wounds. I've never seen him in this condition. "Hang in there, damn it. You better make it. Ian, you hang in there, kid."

I don't hold back. Tears fell down my face. "Damn it. This will not go unanswered. Who did this to you?" I hold his hand, squeezing it and praying that he makes it. We have a lot of enemies, but only one who pulled that motherfucking car out of the family estate.

CHAPTER FIFTEEN

CLAUDIA

I WAKE UP WHEN THE BEDROOM DOOR CLOSES, SO I get up and go to the bathroom. I'm assuming Connor left because I was being a little too intimate. Did he hear what I said before I passed out? Did I say it out loud?

I can't fall in love with my husband. This is temporary. When I come out of the bathroom, I slip my jeans back on, and that's when I hear my phone.

I hope it's Connor calling me and not another cake order. When I look at it, I realize it's my father calling. He hasn't called since the last time that Connor took my phone.

"Hello," I answered with a bit of hesitation.

"I'm surprised you answered and not your husband," my father says. The revulsion shoots from his voice, but I ignore it because he doesn't deserve my respect. Everything sweet and caring between us has ended. I want nothing to do with that man. All I have left for him is contempt.

"Are you calling to congratulate me?" I asked him in an attempt to annoy him, wondering why he dared to call.

"Why would I call you and congratulate you when you are married to a thug?" His disgust is thick on his tongue. A bitter laugh leaves my throat as I listen to his hypocrisy.

"It takes one to know one, doesn't it?" I questioned, allowing a bit of strength to come out. It's a strength that I could have only gathered from being with Connor. He's allowed me to be strong.

"I swear it wasn't like that," he stammers as if he's actually bothered by what happened. It's the first time I've heard his voice falter.

I chuckled again at his denial. "Please, spare me your bullshit. You hate me, and I know it. I don't know if it's because Mom left and you resent me, or if it's something else. Either way, I don't care."

"Claudia, you were named after my mother who I loved and loved you, but.... I resent you because you're not my blood. You're the daughter of my former limo driver."

My cell phone falls from my hand and lands on the bed as my breath rips from my chest. It takes me a moment to respond and scoop up my phone. It can't be true because that would make my life a lie. "What? No, that can't be right," I insist.

"It is. Your mother had an affair with him. He's no longer employed in the state and refused to acknowledge you. I would have taken the bastard to court or divorced her when I learned about it, but would have ruined my career. I was in the middle of a damn re-election run."

My sweet nana wasn't related to me, but shared everything she loved about baking with me. My mind races, spinning with the possibilities. Then it struck me that the DNA test could have been wrong when it came to John. "But that means that you still could be John's dad."

"You did a DNA test between the two of you?" he questions.

"Yes."

"And no one else in their family?" he asks.

"And Connor. It came back that they share the same mother, but John and I are not related."

"That's because Evelyn MacNamara and I had an affair."

"Is that why Mom left?" I ask.

A sigh falls from the other end of the phone. "No. She left because I couldn't handle losing her," he chokes out. "Her death broke me, and I will take down that family at all costs because they stole the love of my life from me." The anger in his voice is vivid, real, and so full of pain.

"Even kill me?" I can't believe what he's saying. My entire life I'd been his good daughter, trying to win his love. It would have never happened because his heart had been broken. I was a child he didn't want by a woman he didn't want. Then, I wasn't even his child.

"I swear you were never meant to be hurt."

"Yes, because shooting up my shop wasn't liable to get me shot."

"I thought the hired gun was an expert marksman. That's what Mirren told me when he picked him out." This whole time, I thought he found out after the fact, not that he was a part of the attack. The sleaze was the orchestrator. I can't wait to tell Connor. He's going to want Nick's head even more than he already does.

He takes a beat and continues. "If I knew he was some scrub off the street, I would have never used him. I just wanted my revenge on the family that let her die." I don't even care that he risked my life. I'm more upset that he wanted Connor dead. My Connor. They loved their mother, and she loved her sons. She would never have wanted that.

"You're the one who let her die. You could have helped her at any time."

He sighs. "She was afraid of him and what he could do. With all her sons, she didn't know how far his loyalty would go."

"No, you're just a coward. I know her sons, and they would have done anything for her, and they would know that she wanted that baby. They said she would have done anything to have that baby. Your baby. A real man would do anything for his family, not destroy it. If you really loved her, you would have done anything for her."

"You have no idea how fucked up the elder Jack MacNamara really is and the depths he'd go to have his way. He never took insults kindly, and he truly hated us."

"Don't make excuses now. Don't call me again." I end the call and walk back into the other room just as Nora's eyes fill the tears and Jack is running out the door. "What's going on?" I ask.

"I'm not sure. Something's happened to Ian," she sobs. I threw my arms around her and hugged her tight. I can't believe this is happening.

"Where's Connor at?" I asked, looking for my husband.

"He went in the ambulance with Ian. Jack's getting a bag for John, and we're heading to the hospital now. Come on, let's go."

"You want me to come?" I questioned.

"Of course—you're part of the family. There's no way in hell you're staying here by yourself," Jack says, coming into the room in a rush with a large bag.

"I'm not alone. There are guards everywhere."

"Connor would kill me if I left you and someone came here to hurt you. Let's go. We need to get to the hospital." I can see the pain etched across Jack's face, the tear stains, and the water in his eyes, so I don't give them any more resistance. It must be terrible right now. I pray that he makes it. Ian and I aren't that close, but he was getting nicer to me. Like the rest, everybody is wary of me because of my father.

I have a lot of information to share, but I don't know if they'll like it. I don't know what any of it means about their mother or their father. A bigger part of me wonders if their mother really died from the effects of childbirth, or if their father took his revenge out on her for the baby.

We hop into the SUV, and other SUVs follow while another one leads. We're not going unarmed or unprepared today. "The house has been monitored. I don't know who did this to Ian, but we'll find out, girls, so just take it easy and relax, okay?" Jack says, trying to reassure us as the silence is pregnant with fear. He takes Nora's hand in his and brings it to his lips, giving her a kiss.

She brushes his jaw. "I love you," she whispers. He squeezes her hand again. God, I wish things were this simple and real between Connor and me. We reach the hospital in record time and rush into the main area before we are directed to a waiting room for the OR area. Pacing there is Connor, who looks completely devastated. I pray that Ian made it here, and he's in surgery and it's not the end.

"What's going on?" Jack asks.

"He's in surgery. They're asking for us to give blood. Apparently, there's a fucking shortage. They'd like to test us."

"Sure. Anything." All four of us adults are brought up to the blood area, and they take samples and test for a possible blood transfusion. Even though I'm not related, my blood type might be a match, or at least a possible donor. I know I'm a possible donor because I know my blood type, but that doesn't mean anything.

The phlebotomist nurse leads us to the special room for donations and says, "You can take a seat and we'll call you as soon as we can, okay? We already have some more O negative blood. However, your brother is going to need a lot more than we have on supply right now. Unfortunately, we had a severe multi-car accident on the expressway with sixteen other people severely injured, so we're asking for donations."

"Fuck. Of all the fucking hospitals," Connor snarls, and we follow his gaze.

We turn around, and there's my father with his security detail and he's staring right at all of us. A gaggle of reporters follow him into the area, which I'm sure isn't safe or allowed. "Governor Saunders, it's a pleasure to have you here. We're glad your people could bring you in to make a donation today," the same woman who spoke to us says. Okay, totally get the PR move, and they need the support. Blood isn't like money; you can't just get anyone to do it easily. "Anything for the people." He gives his killer smile, and then one of the reporters spots me and they all draw their attention and cameras toward me. "Well, your daughter's here making a donation as well," the reporter adds.

"Yes, I am," I answer, giving them a sickly sweet smile, stepping away from my husband and his family to avoid any attention to their situation. "Anything for a good cause, of course. Right, Daddy?"

"Of course, sweet girl." He puts his arm around my waist, and I can feel Connor's eyes boring down on us. "I've taught her well, but it's more because she has a heart of gold."

"Please, this way, Governor Saunders, and we will get you started." He gives me an apologetic look as the reporters are escorted by security. "I'm sorry, but your reporters have to leave now."

I return to my family. "Great job making it look good," Jack says.

"I just didn't want them asking any questions. Although I don't think I can donate given my recent incident."

"We understand," Jack says.

"Are you okay?" Connor asks me. As much as I want to tell him about the conversation with my father earlier, I don't think now is the appropriate time. There's so much about his mother I can't mention. I don't need them to be any more upset than they are already. I guess what they really believe the truth may be is better, but what does it mean? And how could that affect them and how they view their mother?

And what does this mean when it comes to the revenge plan against my father? He is John's dad, after all—his real father. I look over at Jack, and I see the way he cradles his family and the possessiveness he has. What would Jack do if he lost Nora? He would go insane and kill everybody. Except that, being a man in a public position, he wouldn't try to use legal means, and he'd use shady people to hide behind his political persona because Jack was a mobster and had no fear of the repercussions. My dad may not be as tough as Jack, but there were things I didn't understand, and right now looking at the situation, I'm starting to understand that their relationship is complicated.

"Excuse me for a minute. There's something I need to speak to my father about," I state, moving toward the exit.

"I don't think that's smart." Connor is holding onto my arm, refusing to let me go.

I pull it free and stare into my husband's worried yet angry eyes. "He's not going to hurt me in there. I need to know some things. Just so you know, he may just be John's dad for real because I'm not his blood daughter. My mother had an affair, and I'm the daughter of his limo driver."

He raised his brow, staring at me with uncertainty. "How do you know that?"

"He called me while you were gone earlier. I didn't get a chance to tell you. I asked him why he resented me so much, and he told me. It's complicated, but I'm not his real daughter. Give me a moment." I stand on my toes to kiss Connor's cheek and walk away.

He's in a private area cut off with a curtain since he's special, but I walk past everyone. "I need to speak with my father," I tell his security guards who know the drill, and the nurses step away.

"Are you going to use this chance to blow air into my tube here?" he whispers.

"No. Just want to ask you a question."

He looks around and nods. I take a deep breath, wanting to make sure I ask the right one because he's a professional question dodger. "Did you ever try to get her to leave with you?"

He nods. "Yes." An emotion I've never seen from him before happens. His face is contorted with pain. Tears form in his eyes, and not just the crocodile tears he's used for the cameras. No, these are the kind of tears I've never witnessed.

"She was going to leave him. After she had the baby. I wish I had taken her myself, but there was a gubernatorial conference for my re-election that I had to attend. She told me to go, that she would be safe, and I could get her right after. We were wrong. I loved Evelyn Marie so much that I'd do anything for her, including letting her go when I wanted to keep her. You may hate me, and I understand that. Truly, I'm sorry that I couldn't give you the love that you deserved. For that, I'm sorry. But I hope you find that love, and I hope Connor is nothing like his father and is everything that she was."

"Thank you. Thank you for being honest." I kiss his cheek and walk away, tears in my eyes. I wipe them away before I go back and see my husband, who I'm going to say goodbye to now.

I walk up to Connor and say, "I'd like to cancel our contract."

He shakes his head at me. "No fucking way. No fucking way in hell."

"Connor, please. You may hate him, but I don't, and I don't want any part of it." I walk out of the hospital to get some air. As soon as I step outside, I know I made a mistake and want to return to Connor, but I'd said too much when he was already hurting. He didn't need me to make things worse, and I did just that. What a selfish bitch.

The men that work for the MacNamaras are all around. "Mrs. MacNamara, you shouldn't be out here all alone."

"Is there someone who can take me home?" I ask, needing to get far away from Connor. He doesn't need me here right now.

"Yes, I can," he says.

"Thank you." I get in the vehicle and as he pulls out of the lot, I tell him where to take me.

"That's not home, ma'am," he scolds me through the rearview window.

"Technically, it still is my home."

"I don't believe Mr. MacNamara will be pleased."

"I assure you, right now he wants to see the back of me." He gives me a skeptical look and drives on.

"If that's what you wish." It's not. What I want is Connor to really be in love with me the way I love him and for us to put this contract to bed. It doesn't matter to me anymore, but he only wants revenge against my father and a divorce. I can at least give him the divorce.

I sit in silence in the back and think about my bakery that I haven't been in since the shooting. I have no idea what I'm going to be walking into, but I don't really have a choice. I made my decision when I walked out on Connor. I'm glad that I had my purse on me while I was at Nora's.

What am I going to walk into? Have criminals ransacked it? Oh goodness, it's probably a mess and has been looted. I really need security cameras. With the new sales I have planned, I should be able to afford the upgrades.

When we pull up to the building, the wood is gone and the glass has been completely repaired. I'm shocked because it's only been a week and I haven't spoken to the people about repairing it yet. "Thank you for taking me."

"I'll wait until you're inside, Mrs. MacNamara. Holler if anything is wrong."

"I will. Thank you again." I bite my bottom lip and then step out of the back of the SUV.

I enter my apartment from the side because I'm not in the mood to walk through the chaos of the destroyed storefront. When I open my apartment door, it's pretty much just as I left it. Oh my goodness. "All the food," I gasp. All my produce in the fridge must be gross by now.

I don't want to deal with it right now. I strip out of my sweater and toss it to the side. My body and soul ache, and I need a shower. Stripping naked, I turn the water to hot and then wait for it to get heated before climbing in. With the water spraying on me a few minutes later, the heat gives me a bit of relief until I hear, "Couldn't wait to wash me away?"

CHAPTER SIXTEEN

CONNOR

THIS IS THE WORST FUCKING DAY OF MY LIFE. I can't believe shit. I want to go in there and smash his face in, but I need to hunt her down and stop her. Jack comes up behind me as I stare at the empty hallway. "Go after her. We'll watch and keep you posted. There's nothing you can do here. You know surgery is going to last a long time, Brother." Jack hugs me.

"Thanks." I ran after Claudia.

When I get outside, she's gone. I see another one of my guards. "Where the hell is my wife?"

"Tommy took her home," he says. "That's where she wanted to go."

"Okay."

I rush off to my vehicle so I can get to her. Only two minutes into driving home, I get a text message from Tommy. *Taking her to the bakery apartment. She said you'd approve. I'll stay outside.*

Good. Don't leave her. I'll be there soon, and don't tell her I'm coming.

My chest aches when I hear she decided she wanted to go to her apartment and worse, called it home. There's no way she can just get away from me that easily. We have a deal, a contract, and we haven't even met a fraction of it. Yes, her father was a portion of it, but she still had to bake Nora and Jack's wedding cake and so far, it doesn't look like they're getting married any time soon.

I pull up behind Tommy, and he steps out to meet me. "Any issues?"

He shakes his head. "No. She went straight through the side door to the apartment."

"Okay. Good. You can go. I'll deal with my wayward wife."

He nods and then presses his hand on my forearm as I try to turn away. "Sir, just so you know. She said that you would be glad to see the back of her."

"Really?" my brows knit together in surprise.

"Yes. I thought it was odd, but I figure couples have spats. Me and the missus have had our share, and she's gone to her mother's to cool down."

"Yeah. Well, if my wife ever tells you that shit again, don't fucking believe it because her ass doesn't belong anywhere but at home. Her real fucking home."

"Understood."

"Have a good night."

"I'm going to check in with the wife and then go back to the hospital," he says.

I nod and then make my way into her apartment. I've had a copy of her key since the day after she was shot. There was no way I didn't want information on her. Now, it's time to remind her that this contract hasn't gotten to its end date.

I slink into her apartment and hear the shower running. So help me God, now isn't the time for my dick to be this hard. My brother is in the hospital fighting for his life, and she's over there giving me hell.

I push open the bathroom door and stare at perfection. Damn, I have to bite my knuckles before I pounce on her. A low groan escapes her as she rubs her shoulders. My cock swells against my slacks, loving the sound from her pretty lips.

She spreads her legs and the loofa glides lower. "Couldn't wait to wash me away."

She lets out a gasp and turns to face me. "What are you doing in here? How did you get in here?"

"Who do you think had the windows repaired?"

"I appreciate it. I'll have everything out of your home soon." She continues to wash her body, turning away from me in the process, although that doesn't do much good because I love seeing her from behind too. It's like waving a red fucking flag in my face. I'm about to spear her ass.

"What the fuck makes you think any of this is over?" I snap.

"I told you I didn't want this."

"This contract is between the two of us, and I don't recall agreeing to the dissolution. You still owe Nora and Jack a cake," I say, trying to stop her from wanting a divorce.

"We don't need to be married for me to make their cake. I've already agreed to do it, although I don't know when they want to marry." She rinses off and says, "You shouldn't have left the hospital. It's not like we have much to say. We've always said this was temporary."

She turns off the water and then grabs a towel, wrapping it around her perfectly curved body. Her ample breasts hold up her towel, and my bones ache to toss her on the bathroom floor and take her like a savage, reminding her that she's my damn wife and will always be.

"Why are you doing this today?" Of all the days to pick a fucking fight right now isn't it. My brother's on the fucking table and I need my wife by my side.

"I've spoken to my father and have decided he doesn't deserve to die. I might not like him, but I don't want him dead."

"Are you serious? Why are you so damn weak all of a sudden? I knew he would talk you into it. I thought you were strong enough, but he only had to speak sweet words to you, and you'd fall for it," I spat out, anger getting the better of me.

"Please leave, Connor."

"No."

"Get the fuck out. I don't want to see you again. Trust me —if you use sweet words, they won't work. I'm going to pray for your brother's recovery and maybe for your soul because you need it. Now, leave me alone because I'm done."

"Are you serious?"

"I'm so damn serious." She pulls the ring off her finger. "My father told me he hoped you'd be a better husband, someone who deserved me, but maybe the next guy will do the job right."

"I fucking warned you about that. You're my wife," I reminded her for the hundredth time.

She shakes her head. "It was always temporary, Connor. Now leave." I feel like my heart's cracking. I knew I never wanted just temporary, but it seemed she always did. I storm out of there before I fucking say something dumb. Or like even dumber than I already have.

I need a damn drink.

I drive home and as I reach the estate, I see the burned-down house. It's not completely ruined, but I want to see what was there. It's in ruins just like my life.

"Wake up, bro...Wake up...Connor." I scrunch my eyes and flutter them open. I start coughing as I pull myself out of the slumber. "What the hell? Did you really sleep in this pile of rubble all night?"

"How's Ian? God, please tell me something good," I grunt, sitting upright in the mess.

"He's in intensive care, and we can see him later today," he answers.

"Are you serious? That's great news." I smile and hug my brother, but I can't muster more than that. There is nothing left inside me. I thought I'd be fucking over the moon right now, and yet, I need a bottle of whiskey.

"I'm assuming things aren't good with Claudia," he sighs, taking a seat beside me.

"She wants a divorce."

He frowns. "I thought that's what you wanted too."

"It was supposed to be the plan after I killed Saunders." I hoped I could convince her to stay. Maybe she'd see how good we were together and that waking up beside me felt as incredible as it did for me. I loved holding her in my arms every morning.

He crossed his arms. "So what changed her mind? Did you cheat on her?"

"Never."

"Hit her?" A hardened glare comes over his face.

"God, no." I rub my hand over my face. "She talked to Saunders, and he is what changed her mind. I refused to end the contract because I don't want the divorce."

"Does she know that you won't kill Saunders?"

"I…" Are we really fighting about that? No, she doesn't want to be my wife and made that clear, great sex or not. "Shit. I hadn't thought of it, but it doesn't change anything. She wants it over between us."

"No, she doesn't want you to kill her father. Whatever he said changed her mind, but then maybe there's a good reason for it. Honestly, Claudia hates your housekeeper," he says.

"How do you know that?" I asked.

"Nora told me, and that means she's jealous as fuck. At least, that's the vibe that Nora got. She said that she's jealous because your wife has feelings for you."

Even if she did, I managed to fuck that up last night. "Not anymore." I drop my fucking head, kicking the damn box in my father's burned-down garage. When I do, I find a little hatch. "What the fuck?"

"What is that?" Jack says. He pulls on it, and a small little crawl space appears. Inside is a small box that says: *To My Boys* on it.

Dearest Jack, Connor, & Ian,

I love you more than words can say. This hiding spot was built without anyone but the contractor and I being aware of it. So, when you read this letter, I won't be here anymore. I hope I'm not far away, and maybe we'll see each other from time to time and you won't hate me, but there is a chance your father finds me before I can escape with John. There are many things I haven't spoken about, partly because of shame and partly because of fear.

I will always love you boys, but I can't live with your father anymore. He's so evil, and now that I have your brother to care for, I must protect him before it's too late. I can't stay through another lifetime and wait for John to grow up. I must explain something to you. There is a man I met, and we fell in love. He's John's real father.

If I die, please love your brothers as you should and be kind to the little one. He has no part to blame in my choices. I wish I could say more, but your father will be home soon. Hopefully, you will allow me to tell you the truth later.

Love, your mother

"Damn it, I'm going to tear my own balls off." I slap my hand on my head. "Claudia's never going to take me back."

"Why?"

"I fucking said she was essentially weak for believing Saunders's sob story. He might have told her this same fucking story What the hell am I supposed to do?"

"Look, you were upset, Connor. Cut yourself some slack and just remember that you had a right to not buy a word that came from Saunders."

"Of course I was upset. She wanted to divorce me and didn't give a fuck about my damn feelings. God, I sound like a little bitch. Fuck, Saunders told me I didn't know the truth and I knew our sperm donor was lying. You have no idea how much I hurt her."

"Grow a pair and tell her how you feel. Apologize and explain that you didn't mean to be so damn insensitive and that you didn't want to divorce, so you might have been a dick about it. It's not like she doesn't know you're a dick. Hell, the first time I met Nora, I choked her pretty ass and called her some choice words. Granted, I didn't hurt her, but she should have hated me."

"True."

"Look, there's a picture." Inside, there's a picture of my mother at an event and with her is Saunders. He has his hand around her waist like a possessive man. It's an older picture, but I'm not sure when it was taken. I flip it over, wondering the year, but there's no damn Kodak stamp on the back with the date.

"She didn't even write the year on it," I complained.

"Maybe she didn't need to know. If it's when they met, she knew it by heart," Jack says.

"I'm going to go speak to that asshole," I grumbled. As much as I hated Saunders. He had answers that we needed.

"Don't kill him." I take his warning with a hefty laugh because I'm not interested in killing her father unless he gets in my way.

"Hell, I wasn't planning to off that fucker until after your wedding and since that's not happening any time soon, he's safe."

I hug him, and then he adds, "Go shower. You smell like a campfire."

"Good idea."

I shower and as I step out with a towel wrapped around my waist, I find Anna in our bedroom. "What the fuck are you doing in here?"

"I figured since your wife isn't around, you'd need my comfort."

Cain wakes from his spot on the settee. "My wife is all the woman I need. You're fired."

"What? You can't do that. She's nothing to you and it's only temporary."

"Where did you hear that?"

"I heard her speaking to Nora MacNamara," she says, taking another step forward.

"You have one second to get out before I take matters into my own hands," I snarl.

"You should reconsider. It's only a matter of time—"

"Cain, sick." He launches off the settee and right into her. Cain bites her arm, tugging it back and forth. "Excuse me, but I have to change."

Her screams alert the security outside, and they come upstairs to check on me. "I step out of my bathroom in slacks and dress shirt.

"Sorry, but Cain is just disposing of the trash. I want her off my property." I'm livid that she dare come into my bedroom and disrespect my wife.

"Sir, she's lost a lot of blood."

"Not my problem. If she lives, she better keep her mouth shut. If not, Cain can finish his meal."

"I'll be quiet," she cries out.

"Cain release." He does and sits by her.

"I want this room cleaned up. When my wife comes home, I don't want any signs of blood or hints that this tramp was in our bedroom. I should kill her for her disrespect alone."

I call Jack and ask if he'd like to join me when I meet with Saunders. "No, I might kill the prick. The difference in the bakery incident was that you had taken our spot. He would have had someone kill my wife. The only thing saving him is that he's John's dad and I want to know more about his relationship with our mother."

"I understand. I'll let you know what I learn later on."

"Okay. Good luck."

After my talk with Saunders, I needed a drink, but what I really needed was Claudia. It's around ten when I arrive at the bakery, which is still closed, but I see my pretty little wife is bustling around in the front, looking so adorable. I unlock the door, and it dings.

"Connor," she gasps before she turns around.

"That's right, Trouble. I'm here, and I'm not leaving without you."

"Then I suggest you roll up your sleeves because I have a lot of work to do. I planned to bake some cupcakes to take to the hospital today, and they're only half done." She raises her brow at me with one hand on her hip.

"As long as I don't have to eat them," I state.

She gasps, mouth falling open with shock. She points a flat spatula at me, giving me a glare that only turns me on. "You are definitely not a spokesman for me."

I smirk and stalk toward my wife. "You, I'll eat all day long, but I'm not recommending anyone else try."

"But the div—"

"If you use the 'd' word one more time..." I warn her, closing the distance and snatching the damn utensil from her hand and setting it on the counter.

"Di...ck," she finishes. My hand goes to her ass, swatting it before cupping the perfect cheeks.

"You're going to get a dick, all right. Right between those bratty lips of yours."

"You wouldn't." She knows I will and the look in her eyes, screams, no dares me to do it.

"Yes, I would, but first I'll take you in the back area where I feel it's safer. This place isn't giving me the best vibes."

"I got a good vibe upstairs."

"We'll save it for later," I wink and then pull her into my arms. "Claudia, I love you. I'm a fool and I should have told you sooner, but I do love you."

"I love you too."

"I'm not going after your father," I explained. He and I had a long heart-to-heart and although we won't ever be close, we had an understanding.

"I know. He called me," she says, smiling up at me.

"He did?"

"Yeah, he said he put in the good word for you."

I let out a belly laugh. "That's fucked up when I need a good word from that asshole."

"Tell me about it." She tosses her head back with, letting her ponytail swing as she giggles. "So what did you two discuss?"

"Later. I need a kiss from my wife." I cup the back of her head with my fingers sliding up to grasp that amber hair in my grasp. I plant my lips on hers, kissing her furiously. "You're mine forever."

"Forever."

EPILOGUE

CLAUDIA

THE SOUND OF THE BELL BEHIND ME ALREADY tells me there's a customer. But I already know who it is because his presence always is felt.

"What brings you in?"

"I'm in for dessert. The most delicious one you have here."

I continue to fix the display sign, refusing to face my husband and give away my desire. "We have so many kinds," I say.

"There's one I'm looking for specifically. It's the best I've ever had. Every time I have it, it just gets sweeter and sweeter. I seem to not be able to get enough of it."

I turn around and stare at my husband of two years. "Oh, really. I thought you didn't like sweet things."

"Well, there's only one sweet thing I like. Think it's all that sugar you eat."

"Well, I'm kind of busy right now, sir. I think you're going to have to come back."

"Nope. It's closing time, beautiful. I want my cake and my pie." His eyes go directly between my thighs. My husband is such a fucking pervert, and I love every minute of it.

I'm closing this bakery next week. It's time Connor and I start a family of our own, and I can't continue to do this and have a family. I've decided that I'll bake for fun and take online orders only, making them from home. Connor has expanded the kitchen even more so I can still bake. It's amazing, and even Nora loves to come over to try my treats, although she says she has to stay away or she's going to put on too much weight. Jack doesn't mind. He always has his hands on her.

"Mr. MacNamara, you're just going to have to wait."

"You know, I'll just have to take my treat right here." He scoops me up and carries me to the back as I squeal.

"You animal."

He sets me on the steel counter and lifts my skirt, giving me a smile. "You're mine, and I'm obsessed with my wife. I thought you had learned that by now."

Oh, I have. He's certainly proven that this marriage is as real as it gets.

"Hot and fresh," he growled. Dropping to his knees between my legs, he slides my panties off and then presses his face to my cunt.

"Oh my goodness." I damn near hop off the table when his tongue swirls in my hole. I never get enough of him eating me out. My hand thrusts into his hair and pushes his head into my pussy, grinding his face into me. He devours my mound like a hungry man and I lose it, coming on his tongue, shouting his name.

He stands up and fixes my clothes. "It's time to go, Wife."

"What about you?"

"I came for my dessert. Later, I'll be making you so sore that you can't walk, but you have cakes to finish. Let me help, and then we can get out of here."

We clean up inside my apartment upstairs, which is where we usually go for our rendezvous. Three hours later, we left the shop, smiling and satisfied. I'm a happy wife with my insanely handsome and obsessed husband.

THE END

ABOUT THE AUTHOR

Find out more about Carina Blake:
Website: www.carinablake.com
Facebook: www.facebook.com/AuthorCarinaBlake
Instagram: www.facebook.com/AuthorCarinaBlake
Tiktok: www.tiktok.com/@carinablake
Bookbub: www.bookbub.com/profile/carina-blake

ALSO BY CARINA BLAKE

Bratva Royalty:

Ruthless Kingpin

Bratva Prince

Ruthless Prince

The MacNamara Brothers:

Vengeful Reign

Twisted Contract

Stolen Hearts Series:

Stolen Wife

Stolen Dove

Stolen Tutor

Stolen Bride

Standalone:

Vegas Baby